READY, SHIFT, AND GO

BILLIE BLACKWATER, BOOK TWO

KIRA BRINAMON

Published by Blue Unicorn, an imprint of World Weaver Press, LLC
Albuquerque, New Mexico

Cover layout and design by Sarena Ulibarri
Cover images used under license from DepositPhotos.com.

ISBN-13: 978-1734054545

Also available as an ebook.

READY, SHIFT, AND GO

SATURDAY

Even in human form, Billie could usually slink mostly unnoticed among the residents of Juniper, but at the cemetery today, everyone kept turning to look at her. Though maybe it was her boyfriend, Caleb, they were curious about. Only a couple of weeks ago, half the town had seen him get carried off by a winged monster. And yet here he stood, while all those being mourned today had not been so lucky.

Or rather, here he sat, in one of the flimsy folding chairs set up throughout the hillside cemetery. His stitches had been removed, but he still limped and had trouble standing for long. Billie squeezed his hand, wishing she could make the both of them invisible, shield them from the questioning glances of so many of Juniper's locals.

Brock leaned on his crutches beside them, his face twisted with all the grief he hadn't yet processed. He was a friend and co-worker of Caleb's, and his injury had been caused by the monster too, though indirectly. Brock fidgeted with the paper that contained the eulogy he'd written for his wife. Billie pulled her sleeves down over her hands and stared at the ground while more people crowded into the cemetery.

Reverend Provine raised both hands and waited until everyone quieted, then announced, "Friends, we are here today to mourn the loss and honor the lives of several valued members of our community: Daniel Gadbury, Franklin Cokes, Gilbert Gorman, and Toby Moran."

"And Tara," Brock said, loud enough that even more eyes turned their direction.

Reverend Provine nodded and said, "And maybe, though we hope not, Tara Rossman as well."

None of Tara's family was at the funeral—officially she was still only "missing," and her parents and siblings out in Texas had refused to accept that she'd been killed. But Brock knew. Caleb knew. And Billie knew. Tara's mangled body had been buried in the forest, but Brock had bought a small plot in Juniper's cemetery anyway.

After the reverend read some scriptures and led the group through several prayers, he announced there would be one eulogy for each of the dead, delivered by a person who had been close to them. "Mr. Moran, would you please begin?"

Billie glanced up from the ground long enough to watch Elliot Moran step forward. He looked noticeably older than she remembered him, with crow's feet lightly touching the corners of his eyes, and strands of gray wisping through his slicked-back hair. Billie had never known him well, but in high school he'd been the one her peers went to if they needed someone to buy them alcohol or cigarettes, the one who could track down whatever drug they wanted to try. Toby Moran had largely stepped into that role after Elliot left town. He'd moved to somewhere in southern Colorado, though he was still around now and then, often delivering some illicit shipment to Toby or Mouse.

"My cousin Toby was a mean little kid," Elliot started, and the crowd chuckled, some of them nodding. He told a childhood anecdote about his cousin, but Billie had trouble listening. She kept seeing Toby Moran's body in her mind, the shredded viscera of his torso, the blood staining the driveway where she'd found him. She clenched her fists, focused on the flecks of quartz glinting in a rock on the ground.

Elliot finished his story and went back to sit with the rest of his family.

"Mrs. Gadbury?" the reverend invited up the next eulogist, and Billie's fists clenched even harder.

"My son, Daniel, was a such a good boy." She wiped her eyes with a wad of Kleenex.

Your son, Daniel, was a gambling addict and a troublemaker, Billie wanted to say, but of course she didn't. *Your son, Daniel, killed everyone else being mourned at this funeral.*

He had, but Billie was one of the few who knew that. The official story had obscured the truth, blaming all five of these deaths on a man-eating mountain lion. Even most of those who understood that the real culprit was the creature that had attacked the Fourth of July party and flown off with Caleb didn't understand that Daniel *was* the creature. In many ways, he'd been just as much a victim as killer. Daniel Gadbury had become addicted to a strange drug called Scarlet, and it had transformed him into a winged inhuman monster, driven to attack anyone else who had also ingested or possessed the drug. Billie's dad had finally stopped him with a rifle shot, and Daniel had died in the back of the truck before Billie could get him to the hospital.

Was her dad here? Billie lifted her gaze and scanned the faces, but she didn't see him amidst the crowd. Several people met her eyes and quickly flicked their gaze away.

Maybe it was best, Billie thought, that Daniel's family didn't know what had really happened to him. Maybe they would be able to move on with their lives more easily believing he and the others had all been killed by a wild animal. What good would it do them to know the monster their loved one had become?

Mrs. Gadbury started to cry again before she could finish her eulogy for Daniel.

Billie was holding onto Caleb's hand, and she felt his muscles tense as Mitch was tagged next. He was Caleb's dad, and they weren't on good terms. Mitch was also the owner of the Silver Coin Hotel where Billie worked, and he was one of the only people in town who knew she was a shapeshifter. He'd sent her to spy on Daniel Gadbury the night he went to Toby Moran's house demanding more Scarlet, and he'd threatened to expose her abilities and frame her for the deaths if she couldn't figure out who the real killer was.

Mitch surveyed the crowd before he began to speak. "Franklin Cokes and Gilbert Gorman may have been newcomers to Juniper," Mitch said, "But they were good friends of mine." According to some residents of Juniper, Mitch was still a newcomer too, though he'd been there more than a decade and had made a major impact on revitalizing tourism in the small mountain town. Frankie and Gil had been his hired muscle, but they'd fallen victim to Daniel as well. To the gathered crowd, Mitch lamented their loss, and also said some pat condolences about Toby, Daniel, and Tara, mispronouncing Tara's name in the process.

When Mitch had finished his eulogy, Reverend Provine stood again, but Brock loudly cleared his throat.

Caleb gave him an encouraging pat on the back, and Brock hobbled up to the front, leaning on his crutches. Billie offered him a sympathetic smile. His leg had been caught in a rockslide at the quarry where he and Caleb both worked. Not yet fully transformed, Daniel had smelled the Scarlet in Brock's bloodstream and stalked him. If he hadn't slipped and started the rockslide, Brock likely would have been in a casket today as well.

"Tara deserved better than this," Brock started. He leaned heavily on one of his crutches and looked out at the audience.

Then he crumpled the paper he'd been holding and yielded the floor back to Reverend Provine.

The reverend gave a long Bible quote-studded speech about the power of community and the grace of god. "But friends, all of us here, we know what really took these young people from us."

Billie held her breath. The officially accepted story was still that a mountain lion had killed them, before being taken down by local hunters, and any other versions—including the true one—were generally being treated with the veracity of UFO sightings. Billie had delivered Daniel's transformed body to the nearest hospital, but his family never saw the body. The whole incident had been swept under the rug. A second Scarlet Monster had been shot by police in Boulder, but that was being covered up as well, treated like a strange prank. Everyone who had been at the Silver Coin Hotel on the Fourth of July, which included both locals and tourists, had seen Daniel with their own eyes, fully transformed into something with wings, claws, and hard blood-red skin. But the whole thing had happened so fast that no one had managed to film it, and the rationalizations, the misinformation, had spread so fast that no one seemed to understand what they'd seen. Billie stared at the reverend, waiting for him to announce his version of what they all supposedly "knew."

"It was the devil, friends. And I do not mean that in some metaphorical, symbolical kind of way. Those of you who saw what I saw know I mean that the fallen angel himself took physical form here on Earth."

Billie tried to bite back a groan, but it still rumbled in the back of her throat. She caught more than a couple of furtive glances in her direction. This time, she was sure they *were* directed at her. The rumors that her mother had been a witch meeting with the devil in the forest had never fully died away. Or maybe had been rekindled by this recent manifestation of what *did* appear to be a devil, if you didn't know that it was really a person who had taken too much of a strange drug that forced them to transform. Even if the reverend and his followers knew the truth, it probably wouldn't change their minds.

"I won't say any more about that here," the reverend said, "out of respect for these mourning families. But if you want to know more about what needs to happen to prevent the devil's return, I'll be hosting some special gatherings at the church. I hope to see you there."

Eventually, three caskets were lowered and buried. Daniel's family held onto the urn that contained his ashes. Maybe these victims could rest, now. Billie hoped their ghosts hadn't been trapped in this world the way she knew some were.

The crowd gradually dispersed, emptying out of the small cemetery. Caleb started to hobble toward the car, but Billie squeezed his arm and said, "I'll catch up with you in a minute." He glanced toward the gravestones and nodded. He understood what she needed to do, she was sure. Billie waited until a few more people cleared out, and then she slowly made her way across the cemetery toward a headstone near the fence.

The name Valerie Blackwater stared back at her from the weathered stone. No "beloved wife and mother," no porcelain photograph like some of the others had. Just the name, and two dates. Billie realized with a start that her mother had only been thirty-three when she died. Billie herself was almost twenty-six; it wouldn't be that long until they were the same age. She shook her head. The realm of adulthood her parents had occupied still felt like something distant: an alien and unattainable way of living. Part of her was still stuck as that twelve-year-old kid who had watched her mother die when her father shot a mountain lion that wasn't really a mountain lion at all. Maybe always would be stuck that way.

Billie knelt in front of the gravestone. She reached out and used her thumb to smear away a pentagram someone had drawn. At least it was only chalk. Some of the other vandalisms from years past had faded by now to only a speck of paint, a slight discoloration on the stone. When she'd visited this grave the first time, a year after her mother's death, the things people had done to the gravestone had upset her so much that she'd never come back. Not until now. She smudged the chalk until it was only a white smear, and then pulled some weeds from around the stone's base and tossed them away.

Billie stood, brushing the dirt from her hands, picking some stray grass seeds from her jeans. Two kids, around seven or eight years old, lurked a few rows over, whispering and pointing at her.

Catching her eye, one of them stepped bravely forward and said, "My mom said your mom was a witch."

Billie sighed. "Who's your mom?"

The boy shook his head. Didn't matter, Billie decided. She thought one of the boys was Elliot Moran's kid, but she didn't recognize the one who had spoken. The list of locals who *wouldn't* tell their kids that was likely shorter than the list who would. It still brought an angry flush to her cheeks, though.

"Do you believe in witches?" she asked the boys.

They shrugged, looked at each other and giggled. She moved slowly toward them, placing her hands on top of the large headstone they had tried to hide behind.

Billie closed her eyes, and limited the folds of her shift to that vertical pupil slit and yellow iris of her bobcat form. Opening her eyelids, she leaned in toward the boys and said, "Tell your mom I said 'boo!'"

The boys gasped and staggered backward, stumbling over each other to run back to the group of adults who lingered on the far side of the cemetery.

Maybe that had been a bad idea, Billie thought. Perpetuating the rumors. But it had felt good to give them a scare, a little bit of revenge she'd never been brave enough to give the peers who had tormented her through her own childhood. And because they were kids, no one would believe what they said they'd seen.

Billie looked across the cemetery. There was no way to the parking lot that didn't involve walking past the kids again, and probably their parents. So instead, she hopped the cemetery fence and disappeared into the forest. She pulled out her phone and sent Caleb a text: *Meet me @ Silver Coin.* She needed to talk to Mitch anyway, take care of a few things so that she'd be able to leave town tomorrow.

Her dad had said he knew some people down in Durango who were shapeshifters like her, and since she'd heard that—and since she'd realized she could leave Juniper without losing her powers—she'd been unable to think of anything else. She hiked up a columbine-covered hill and navigated through a large aspen grove, crossing a hiking trail, to make her own trail over to Juniper's only hotel.

Caleb swiped away the text and sighed. He was disappointed, but honestly not surprised. Of course she would ditch him. Of course she would ask him to go pick her up at the one place in town he'd just as soon never set foot in again. He'd managed to get through this group funeral without interacting with his dad, but if he showed up at the hotel, Caleb might not be able to avoid him, and that was likely to lead to a fight. It almost always did.

Before he could make it all the way to the car, Reverend Provine stepped in front of him.

"Mr. Mulligan."

Caleb hated it when people called him by his last name. He'd joked that if he and Billie ever got married, he was going to take her last name. He wasn't so sure it was really a joke. Caleb leaned on the hood of someone else's car, his left leg throbbing.

"I was really hoping," the reverend was saying, "that you'd be willing to stop by one of those gatherings I mentioned. As the only one of us who has faced this demon head-on and survived, your insights would be *most* valuable."

Hell no, I'm not joining your witch hunting cult, was what Caleb wanted to say.

"Yeah, sure, I'll consider it," was what he mumbled instead, and that seemed to satisfy the reverend for now. Enough to leave him alone, anyway.

Caleb spotted Brock and Joaquin a couple of rows over. "Hey, you wanna go get a drink?" he shouted at them.

Brock gave a thumbs up, and by the time Caleb hobbled all the way to the car, several of his friends were ready to jump in with him. There were only two places in town to go: the bar at the Silver Coin, and Fred's Bar and Grill on Miners Avenue. He drove to Fred's. He hung out with Brock and the other guys for a while, until Billie texted him again: *Come pick me up?*

He considered telling her "no." It was barely over a mile to walk from the Silver Coin back to their cabin—which she did all the time—and it was broad daylight and good weather. But eventually he gave in and sent back *Otw*. Brock said he'd get a ride home with one of his cousins, and Caleb got back into the car.

At the Silver Coin, he parked at the edge of the surface lot that overlooked the lake, then texted that he was outside. Just because he was here didn't mean he had to go inside. A deer lapped at a shallow part of the lake. It was a little too far away to tell for sure, but Caleb thought the animal looked ragged, unhealthy, like maybe it had a case of mange. A group of people approached the shore, and the deer bolted away. They held hands in a circle. *Cult's already formed*, Caleb thought cynically, but then he realized it was Daniel's family. After a moment, they lifted their heads and let go of each other's hands. One of them opened the urn that contained Daniel's ashes, and the gray dust fluttered out, dappling the lake.

Billie opened the passenger door and slid in, chirping, "Thanks."

Caleb glared over at her as he started the car.

"What?" she said. "I needed to check on a few things and make sure everything was covered so I can go on my trip."

My trip. Caleb pulled out of the parking lot with a little more acceleration than was strictly necessary.

"And why is it," Caleb said, an edge to his voice, "that you have to go on *your trip* right now?"

Her face crumpled in confusion. "Well, if I wait much longer, it will be Labor Day, and that's always busy at the hotel, and then Kim's got maternity leave coming up after that, and I don't want to wait until *winter* when the roads are awful. So, yeah, right now is the only time I've really got."

Caleb said nothing.

"Wait, are you mad at me?"

She'd finally noticed. "You tell me for *years*," Caleb said, "that you can't leave Juniper. Then the second you find out you can, you leave it without me."

"That's not..." she started. "I just found out there's a whole group of people that are like me, and I might be able to find out answers about my mom, about myself. Can't you understand how much I need that?"

He did, actually, but what killed him was how she'd cut him out of the experience completely, declaring one day that her dad was going to take her to Durango. No discussion, no chance for him to go along or be involved in any way.

"Guess I can't understand," he said instead, his ears burning. The only reason he stayed in this awful town was so he could be with her, and now she was leaving and he was going to be stuck here without her. *Only a few days*, she'd said, but would it be, really?

He parked in front of the cabin and got out, slamming the car door behind him. Billie stepped out too and held out her hand.

"Give me the keys."

Another demand.

"Why?" Caleb barked. "You decide you're going to leave today instead?"

"No, there's just something I need to do."

She grasped for the keys and he pulled them out of her reach.

"You want the keys?" he said. Then he leaned back and hurled the keys like a baseball over the top of the car and across the street. They landed on the far sidewalk with a clink. "Good, go get them."

Billie's mouth dropped open and she stared at him.

"Real mature," she said over her shoulder as she went to retrieve them.

Caleb braced on the porch railings and hefted his injured leg up each step, and it was only once he reached the door and Billie started the car and took off with a lurch that he realized the house key was on that same key ring. He was locked out.

"Shit," he muttered. The back door was probably unlocked. It usually was. But that meant lugging his bum leg back down the stairs and around to the back. He plopped down into one of the plastic porch chairs, trying to let his leg stop aching and his face stop burning before he made that effort.

Yeah, that was stupid. He knew it, but he was hurting in more ways than one, and the hurt made stupid decisions come easily.

Caleb was being an asshole. Billie understood why he wasn't happy about her leaving town, but couldn't he understand that this was something she needed to do? Besides, it was only going to be a few days. She hadn't thrown a fit like this when he'd left for college and been gone for months at a time.

She drove through town and along a street that wound up into the mountains, to an area called Shadow Ridge. What Caleb wanted was for the two of them to leave Juniper for good. Fine. Now that she knew she could shift outside of what she'd always thought of as her territory, there was really only one thing tying her to this town anymore. If she could find some resolution to that, then maybe she could do what Caleb wanted. They could leave, move to some other town and start fresh. Free of Mitch, free of the limited opportunities of this place, free of the constant reminders of bad memories. But she couldn't do any of that if her mother's ghost was still stuck here. If she was stuck in Juniper, then Billie was too.

Maybe she could talk to her mother's ghost, just once, and—how had the owner of the Enchanted Mountain Metaphysical Shop put it?—*help her move on.* Then they would both be free.

The house on Shadow Ridge was for sale, and had been sitting vacant for several months. Billie didn't have a key, but she didn't need one. Last time she'd come up here, she'd seen nothing inside the house, but the rocking chair on the back porch had turned ice cold and moved on its own to warn her when the Scarlet Monster was lurking in the forest behind the house. Billie parked the car and stepped out. The house was in good shape: recently painted, windows clean, driveway clear of the trash or rusting machinery that littered many of the lived-in houses nearby. The yard was a scatter of wildflowers and grasses that wrapped in a wide perimeter around the house, pine trees beyond that. A bird had built a nest in the rain gutter. There was no bird in it—probably forced to abandon what was no longer a safe location during the heavy rains a couple of weeks ago—but the nest, at least a remnant of what it had once been, remained lodged there, hanging over the gutter's rim.

Billie went around the back and climbed the three narrow steps up onto the porch. She sat, her back leaning against the wooden slats of the porch, facing the rocking chair. All she wanted was one conversation. No, that wasn't true. She wanted the thirteen years of conversations that she'd had to miss, and thirteen more after that. But she'd settle for one, if it could bring something like closure to both of them.

The last time she'd been here, a woman named Chloe had been with her, and they'd both seen the rocking chair move. At the Fourth of July event, Chloe had told her, *"I think you should go back up there. Like, soon. I get the sense that she really has something important she needs to tell you."*

Chloe claimed to be psychic, but Billie doubted she was trained the way Heather, the owner of Enchanted Mountain Metaphysical Shop, was. Chloe had surely picked up on *something*, but what if what she'd sensed was that Billie's *dad* had something important to tell her? He had—he'd needed to tell her that he'd met other shapeshifters, that he could take her to them. Billie didn't know anything about being psychic, but that seemed like an easy enough signal to misinterpret: a parent had something important to tell her, and Chloe only knew about Billie's mother. Still, Billie held out hope that her mom *did* have something to say.

She tried waiting quietly on the porch, hardly daring to breathe, making herself as still as possible so the ghost would feel safe coming out into the light. When that didn't work, she alternated between asking, calling, begging, crying, and pleading for her to appear. Then she tried waiting again.

After a while, Billie laid her clothes in a pile on the porch steps the way she and her mother used to when she was a kid, and shifted to bobcat form. The colors of the world changed and the air came alive with all the forest scents. She paced the perimeter of the yard, wondering if her mother might appear in the form of a ghostly mountain lion rather than a woman. But no ghosts of any shape appeared, so she shifted back to human form, got dressed, and then waited some more.

Her stomach rumbled, and she was just about to give up and go home for the night when a cool breeze washed over her, raising goosebumps across her arms and neck. A voice on the wind whispered a single word: "Sybil." Billie's eyes widened. That was her legal name, but she'd never gone by it, not even in school. Most people didn't even know it.

"Mom?" she whispered, throat cracked and dry.

Laughter rippled through the air, and oh, Billie definitely knew that laugh. But then it faded, and the cool breeze became the stale warm air of late summer once again. Billie waited until sunset, but she saw no more signs, heard no more voices. Sunset faded to dark, and she fell asleep on the back porch of her childhood home, still waiting, still waiting.

SUNDAY

Billie woke up sore from sleeping on the hard slats, with a couple of splinters stabbing her face. Disoriented, she rolled over and sat up with a jolt, blinking into the sunlight.

"What time is it?" she asked, though there was no one there to answer. She pulled out her phone, but the battery had died. In any case, it had been dark the last time she remembered, which meant now it was morning. Morning of the day she was supposed to start her trip to Durango with her dad. She scrambled to her feet and stumbled toward the car, hand to her head to still the sudden rush.

She parked in front of the cabin. Her dad's truck wasn't there yet; at least there was that. Maybe she still had time to get packed before he showed up. She put the key in the lock, turned and pushed, and the door stuck. Had Caleb turned the deadbolt too? He almost never did that. She fumbled with the key and unlocked the deadbolt. This time, the door opened.

Caleb sat on the couch, his injured leg propped up on the coffee table, arms crossed.

"Oh," she said. "Hi."

He just glared at her while she shut the door behind her.

"Have a nice night?" he asked after an awkward moment, and the sarcasm in his tone reminded her uncomfortably of Mitch. He'd never really resembled his dad before, but now it was pretty clear.

"Um," Billie said. She opened her mouth to tell him about the ghostly voice she'd heard, but then anger flared through her. He'd been rude to her almost non-stop for the last several days. Her experiences with her mother's ghost were personal, sensitive. She wanted to trust him with them, but right now she really didn't. She didn't trust him at all.

So instead, she crossed over to the bedroom and started shoving clothes into a backpack. Toothbrush, hairbrush, socks... what else did she even need? Billie hadn't gone on an overnight trip out of town since... well, *ever*. Only a couple of daytime field trips when she was in school. Those were the times when her mother had scolded her that she couldn't shift outside of Juniper, mistakenly leading her to a belief that she wouldn't physically be able to, and might break something if she tried. It wasn't until she'd shifted to fight the monster at an old timber mill outside of Juniper that she'd realized she wasn't limited by territory. Billie stuffed what she thought she might need into the bag and zipped it shut.

Outside, a truck rumbled up to park on Miners Avenue in front of the cabin. Billie glanced out the window to confirm it was her dad.

"Are you sure you want to do this?" Caleb asked. His voice was low, hostile.

"No, I'm not sure," she admitted. "But I want to find answers. And he says there are people like me in Durango."

Shapeshifters, she meant, and they both knew it, though Billie still had trouble saying the word out loud, even in the privacy of their own house. Which wouldn't even be their house for much longer, since she'd agreed to sell it to a developer in order to save Caleb from the monster. But Billie couldn't even bring herself to think about that right now. One crisis at a time, and at the moment, the most pressing one was the prospect of spending six hours in a car with her dad. The man who had accidentally shot her mother, thinking he was shooting a mountain lion. The man who had helped defeat Daniel Gadbury after he'd transformed into a demon-like monster. And the only living family she knew. Although she and her dad had had something of a reconciliation, the fact remained that he had killed her mother, accident or not. This was going to be, by far, the most time she'd spent with him since he'd been released from prison.

Billie leaned over to kiss Caleb goodbye, but his mouth was hard, and he kept his arms crossed.

"You'll still be here when I get back, right?" Billie asked, fearing the answer.

"I don't know, Billie. I just don't know."

Billie stood in the middle of the living room for an awkward moment, searching for something to say, blinking back tears. Things had been so good between them. Their time had been constrained by Mitch's demanding schedule, but they'd cherished every second they managed to steal together. But now—couldn't he understand how important this was to her?

Her dad honked the truck horn and Billie let out a breath.

"I love you," she said.

He didn't say it back.

Billie slung the backpack over her shoulder, steeled herself, and walked out the cabin door.

The truck her dad drove was at least a couple of decades old, and several dents pocked the sides. The white paint had been scraped off to the primer in some spots, when you could even see the paint for the mud splashes. The passenger side rearview mirror was twisted at an odd angle, as though it had been hit by another vehicle and never repaired.

"Ready?" her dad asked.

"As I'm going to be," she said.

She tossed her backpack into the bed of the truck and he used a bungee cord to strap it in next to his suitcase. Billie tried not to think about the last time they'd secured something in the back of a pickup truck, but the image flashed through her mind anyway: the Scarlet Monster, wheezing its last few breaths in the bed of Mitch's truck, claws opening and closing as though reaching for anything that might help him survive. Billie slid onto the vinyl seat in the truck's small cab, and took one last look back toward Caleb and the cabin before the truck lurched into motion.

Six hours of driving together. That was going to be challenging, but at least once they got to Durango, she wouldn't be alone with him anymore. She'd be meeting new people, learning new things about her abilities. With luck, she'd find out something about where her mother had come from. She knew nothing about her mother's past or family. Maybe these people knew them. Maybe they *were* them.

At first, she and her dad managed some small talk. As they wound through the switchbacks out of Juniper, her dad pointed out a cloud formation and they talked about the weather, about how much the seasonal patterns had changed since Billie was a kid, about a forest fire up north that had finally been contained. Billie said the truck seemed to be running well, and they talked about the local mechanic who had helped him out with it, a man named Ned who had been letting her dad stay with him for the last couple of weeks.

By the time they reached Frisco, only about forty miles from Juniper, the small talk had fizzled away. Billie stared in silence as they passed by the hospital where they'd taken Caleb after he'd been attacked, carried off by the winged monster because he'd taken a vial of Scarlet away from a friend. This was the farthest from Juniper she'd gone as an adult. Each revolution of the truck's wheels now pulled her further into the unknown.

As they passed through Breckenridge, Billie figured out how to plug her phone into the truck's cigarette lighter to charge. It was just a simple flip phone, capable of calling and texting, but lacking all the apps and internet access that nearly everyone else had. The screen came to life and she saw the list of missed calls from the night before.

Caleb had tried to call her five times while she waited for her mother's ghost on the Shadow Ridge porch. She wasn't sure how to feel about that. Was it because he cared or because he wanted to control her? He'd never been particularly controlling before, but Mitch was, and she'd just seen how quickly he could unconsciously take on Mitch's tendencies.

Billie watched the landscape through the window. The pine-covered peaks, the aspen groves, the grassy meadows where cattle and deer mingled—all of it looked similar to the territory she knew, and yet it was all brand new and strange, the same elements rearranged into different patterns. Her dad was that way, too. Some things about him were achingly familiar: certain gestures and intonations that she remembered so clearly from the time before her world had shattered, even some that she'd unconsciously picked up and replicated herself. And yet, she didn't know him at all. For thirteen years, he'd been gone, and their lives had been so vastly different.

That's what Caleb was actually upset about, she realized. They already had such little time together, but for the next few days they wouldn't even have those precious hours in the early morning and the afternoon that they could normally steal. And she'd be having new and different experiences that he wouldn't be a part of. Maybe, she thought, if she made an effort to share things with him about the trip along the way, he'd relax somewhat. It could become more of a joint experience, even if he wasn't with her. She tried to take a picture of the passing landscape with her phone's camera, but it came out as a blur. She sent it to Caleb anyway. He didn't respond.

Around Fairplay, which was wide open agricultural land with mountain peaks so far in the distance they were small on the horizon, Billie commented, "It hardly looks like we're in the mountains anymore."

Her dad said nothing. His jaw was tense, and she couldn't see his eyes behind the big mirrored sunglasses. This was probably just as awkward for him as it was for her. He'd been trying to reach out to her for months, but now that they were together, it seemed he didn't know what to say.

"How much longer 'til we get to Durango?" Billie asked.

"About four hours."

Four hours. Billie fidgeted uncomfortably in her seat. Amazing how leaving Juniper could make her feel more trapped than when she'd thought she was stuck there. They needed something to fill the tense silence.

"Tell me about these people we're going to meet?"

"Well, there's Stan Lesnik," he said. "He runs a mobile blade-sharpening business that contracts with a bunch of local construction companies. His wife Helen. She was a teacher, but I think she'd just retired when I was there. I met most of their kids—can't remember everyone's names, though. Probably recognize them when I see them." And then he started to repeat the story of how he'd entrusted one of his friends in prison with the truth that the mountain lion he shot in his backyard had transformed back into his wife. This friend had told him of a family of people who could transform into bears and deer, and when he got out, he went to meet them himself.

"Did they know Mom?" she asked.

A twitch rippled over his face. "I never asked," he admitted after a long moment.

Billie was exasperated. "How could you never ask?" He didn't answer, and another long silence descended.

Fine. She didn't know what to say to him, what to ask, which wounds she was okay with poking at. If he had something to say, then he could say it. Otherwise, she was content to just watch the ever-changing landscape scroll by, absorb the details of this outside world she'd never glimpsed before.

Caleb had waited up all night for Billie to come home from wherever she'd run off to, and now that she'd come and gone so quickly, the exhaustion of his anger and the long night overtook him. He fell asleep on the couch with the TV on and woke up disoriented. Some 90s action movie played on the screen, so it was probably the sirens and gunshots from that had woken him, he decided. He shut the TV off and was about to head into the bedroom when a prim tap-tap came from the front door. He pulled on a shirt and opened the door, rubbing the sleep out of his eyes.

Robyn Applebaum stood there with a briefcase. "I didn't realize two in the afternoon would be an early morning for you," she snipped. Without asking if she could come in, she pushed her way inside and plopped the briefcase on the small round kitchen table.

Caleb ran a hand through his messy hair and leaned against the doorframe, still feeling groggy and in need of a pain pill, not really comprehending what Robyn was doing in his house.

"I finally have an offer everyone's going to be happy with," Robyn said as she unloaded papers onto the table. "Oh! It's going to be amazing. Picture this: totally renovated shop fronts all along Miners Avenue, new restaurants, and an Old West-style hotel and spa. Massages, hot tubs, themed rooms. It's going to bring *so* much business to Juniper."

"Wait," Caleb said. "So you're tearing down *actual* Old West buildings to build...an Old West-themed spa."

"Oh, don't say it like that." Robyn flicked her hand. "We're meeting a modern market for authentic historical experience. No one wants to stay in these dilapidated old shacks. Um, no offense." She looked around as though searching for something about the cabin to compliment to make up for her insult. Apparently finding nothing, she frowned down at the papers she'd spread all across the table. "Anyway, I need a couple of signatures from Billie and we can get this whole deal finalized."

"Billie's not here," Caleb said.

"Oh! Is she over at the Silver Coin? I was just there talking to your dad. I must have missed her."

"No, she left town."

Robyn stared at him like he'd just started speaking Klingon.

Caleb shrugged. "She's not here. She left town, for a few days, at least."

Robyn scoffed. "What do you mean, she left town? Billie doesn't go anywhere, everyone knows that."

"She went on a road trip with her dad."

"With… her dad." Robyn sighed. "Look, if she's trying to back out of the arrangement we made, the two of you should at *least* try to get your excuses straight—"

Caleb hobbled back to the couch and fished his phone out from between the cushions while Robyn ranted. He pulled up the picture Billie had sent him. It was a blur of landscape, but it was landscape outside of Juniper. He turned the screen toward Robyn.

"What?" She squinted at the image. "What is this? This could be anywhere."

"She's out of town. All of this—" He gestured toward the stacks of papers "—is going to have to wait until she gets back."

"Which will be when?"

Caleb had asked Billie the same thing and gotten a vague, open-ended answer. Mitch had given her a week off. Whether or not she planned to spend that whole week down in Durango depended on what she found down there, she'd said. Caleb half expected to get a call at some point telling him she wasn't coming back at all.

"Sometime next week, probably," he told Robyn.

She huffed and started stuffing the papers back into her briefcase. "There are other people involved in this deal, you know. I have deadlines, and—ugh! I can't believe how selfish she's being."

On that, Caleb agreed, but he kept his mouth shut. Absently, he picked up one of the papers, some contract with highlighted signature areas. The name on it read, "Sybil Blackwater."

"Who the hell is Sybil?" Caleb muttered. Billie's grandmother, maybe? She'd willed the cabin to Billie when she died, but would it still be under her name?

"That's Billie's full name," Robyn answered, snatching the contract from him and slamming it into the briefcase with all the others.

Really? Caleb frowned. They'd been together for six years and she'd never bothered to tell him her real name? He was pretty sure he'd asked her one time, when they were first getting to know each other, if "Billie" was short for something. She'd told him no.

"You tell her," Robyn said, snapping the briefcase shut, "that I have another client interested in the Shadow Ridge house, and I'm not going to make any more concessions for her if she can't even meet me partway on the basics."

The Shadow Ridge house—Billie's childhood home, where Caleb knew she'd recently had an experience that suggested her mother's ghost might be there. Had she been trying to buy it? Secrets upon secrets. He felt like he already was losing touch with who his girlfriend really was.

On the one hand, he understood Billie's need to try to communicate with her mother's ghost. He sympathized with that, he really did. If he'd had the chance to speak with his own mother, who had died of cancer when he was in middle school, he would have done almost anything to see her one more time. On the other hand, if Billie sold this cabin but bought another one down the road, nothing substantial would change about their life. Caleb couldn't bear the thought of staying in this town forever. He'd made so many sacrifices to be with her, and now that she knew leaving town didn't affect her ability to shapeshift, they had a chance to go somewhere else and make a better life. Together. That wasn't going to happen if she bought an old house in the same town without even asking his opinion.

"I'll tell her," he mumbled.

Out on the porch, Robyn turned and gave him a once-over, her eyes sweeping from his bare feet up to his messy hair. "You can do better than her, you know," she said before she turned on her heel and stomped back to her car.

"We're about ten miles out from Durango," Billie's dad told her. "Should be a turn coming up."

He motioned toward the maps he'd printed out at Juniper's tiny library, which they'd used to navigate this far. She reached down and snatched up the crinkled papers from the floorboard. Her neck was stiff and her hips and lower back ached. They'd stopped only once during this long drive. She couldn't remember ever having to sit in one spot for this long before. It was awful, and she was ready for the drive to be done.

Reading off the papers, she called out turns and street names that took them well off of the main roads, until they were bumping along a dirt road a lot like the one that had taken them to the old timber mill where they'd had the final showdown with the Scarlet Monster. But this road went on longer than that one had, cutting through a muddy canyon.

"Isolated," Billie commented. Of course, if they really were a family of shapeshifters, it made sense they'd want their own space, as wild as possible.

"We're almost there. I recognize this area now."

After a few more minutes, her dad made another turn onto an unmarked road, unprompted by the printed directions. A metal gate stood open, the chain coiled on the ground.

"That's strange," he said.

"They know we're coming, though, right?" Billie said. "So they'd leave it open for us."

Her dad said nothing. As he drove through the gate, she said, "You *did* tell them we were coming." But she knew he didn't have a phone, and he'd never asked to use hers or Caleb's. "Is it safe to just drive up here?"

"Yeah," he said, sounding like he was feigning more confidence than he felt. "What's the worst that can happen?"

"Uh, you want a list?" Billie said. Her breath was getting shorter, her heartbeat quickening.

"It'll be fine, Stan knows me."

Billie shook her head. It seemed very bad form to show up unannounced, and Billie was starting to doubt her dad was as close with these people as he had insinuated.

A two-story wooden house came into view, with dark wood siding and a peaked roof. A crew cab truck was parked in front. Half a dozen chickens pecked at the ground. The door to their coop, just to the left of the house, had been left open.

Her dad parked next to the other truck and stepped out. Billie hesitated, taking a long breath before she joined him. She had so many questions to ask. She couldn't believe that she was finally going to meet more people like herself. Were they really, though? And would they accept her? Billie took one more breath and then opened the truck door. She closed it softly behind her, and followed her dad up the steps to the wide, covered porch.

He knocked on the door, four strong, urgent taps. While they waited for an answer, Billie looked around. The wheels of the truck they'd parked next to were turned sharply, and from this side, she could see that the driver's side door had been left open. Shirts and overalls swayed in the wind on a clothesline, but some of the clothes had blown off and littered the ground. The ones still hanging were spattered with mud. One shoe lay on its side at the edge of the porch, the other half of the pair nowhere to be seen.

Something wasn't right.

Her dad knocked again, but no one came to the door. Maybe they'd heard someone driving up uninvited, and they'd all shifted and scattered into the forest? Billie scanned the windows for fluttering curtains, any signs someone might be peeking out. No movement at all. She turned in a circle, studying the perimeter, the forest surrounding them.

Billie pulled out her cell phone. Only one bar, but that was about all she usually had in most of Juniper, too.

"You have a number for any of them? Stan, maybe?" Her dad had said he was a bear shifter, and the patriarch of this family.

Her dad thought for a second, and then rattled off a number. Billie punched it in.

A second after she heard the ring on her end, it echoed inside the house. She let it ring a few times, listening for any signs of movement inside, maybe someone waking up to go answer. Nothing. The voicemail notification informed her the mailbox was full. She hung up.

Her dad turned the doorknob, and it swung open, unlocked. Billie followed him inside, the hairs on the back of her neck rising.

"Hello?" he shouted. "Anyone home? It's Keith Blackwater. You told me to come back any time, remember?"

Ants crawled over a plate of half-eaten pancakes on the kitchen table. Another plate lay in broken shards on the floor. Billie followed her dad into a living room, where some *Popular Mechanics* magazines had spilled off of the coffee table onto the floor. Water ran inside a small bathroom to the side of the living room. Billie knocked lightly on the door frame before poking her head in. The bathroom was empty, light on and sink overflowing. She reached toward the running faucet, then thought better of it and grabbed a towel, using that to turn it off.

No fingerprints, she thought. *Since I've clearly found myself in a crime scene. Again.*

There was one distinct difference between this and the grisly scene she'd encountered at Toby Moran's house, though. No bodies.

At least, not yet. Billie braced herself as she entered each new room, expecting to stumble upon death and destruction around every corner. There were signs of struggle, but no blood, and no corpses. She wandered back toward the living room. An odd bitter smell lingered throughout the house, something Billie couldn't identify, at least with her human senses. Her dad had climbed the stairs to the second level, and he clomped back down now, shrugging.

"I don't know what happened, but ain't nobody here. I don't like this, baby doll, not at all. We should go."

Billie started to nod, but it turned into a shake. "Wait," she said, though her throat felt tight around the word. "I can... maybe if I shift, I can figure out... something."

"What, like from smells?"

"Yeah, scent trails, residual chemicals. Things we can't see. There's something odd in the air, but I can't tell what it is."

"Okay. So..." He hooked a thumb toward the front door where they'd entered. "You, uh, want me to wait outside then?"

The thought of being trapped in this house alone made it hard to breathe. But she also wasn't going to strip and shift in front of her dad.

"Um, wait here, maybe?" She pointed back toward the bathroom. "I'll change in there."

Change, like she was just putting on another set of clothes.

"Sure, sure." He sat on the larger of the two couches, and Billie stepped back into the bathroom, leaving the door open a crack so she could nose it open in her bobcat form. She slid off her shoes and stood on top of them, rather than standing barefoot on this unfamiliar floor, then unbuttoned her pants, pulled off her shirt, and laid all her clothes neatly on top of the toilet seat. She stared at her face for a moment in this stranger's mirror. Then, she closed her eyes, envisioned the form, prompted the folds that would change her human body into a bobcat.

And nothing happened.

Billie peeked her eyes open, looking down at the splotches and freckles of her bare human arms. Goosebumps dimpled her skin, but it didn't ripple. Normally, it was easiest to shift when she felt scared. It had even happened a couple of times by accident. Most people had fight or flight instincts, but her body offered another option: shift. This abandoned house and whatever had chased off the people she'd hoped to meet certainly inspired plenty of fear. So why couldn't she shift?

She closed her eyes again, concentrated, initiated the process she'd gained conscious control of when she was still a toddler. Set the creases in the paper, so to speak, that would fold her into the shape that was so natural she hardly ever had to think about it this precisely anymore. But still, nothing changed. Her human body was as rigid as a cardboard doll.

Billie reached for her clothes, started pulling them back on with shaking hands.

She'd shifted outside of what she'd thought was her territory, twice, dispelling the belief she'd always had that her powers were limited to Juniper. Her dad had assured her that these people he'd met—these people whose house she was standing in now—had told him that territory wasn't a factor the way she thought it was. What if he had been wrong? She'd come hundreds of miles, well and truly out of her territory this time. And here, she couldn't shift.

She got dressed and shoved her shoes back on. The heel was smashed down on the left one, but she didn't bother to fix it. Billie nudged the bathroom door open with her elbow and beelined for the front door.

"Did you… did you already do it?" her dad asked from the living room.

"We need to leave, now," she said.

"But I thought…"

"We need to go," she repeated, and pushed open the front door.

The chickens squawked and fluttered as she hurried past them. Her dad closed the door behind them and then slid into the truck. Billie yanked at her shoe until she fixed the folded-over heel, then rubbed her hands across her arms, trying to smooth away the goosebumps as the truck jounced down the driveway, away from the house.

A little way down the road, the truck's tire hit a large rock in the road, and the jolt bounced Billie practically up to the roof of the truck cab. Her skin rippled.

"Stop the truck," she said.

"Huh?"

"Stop the truck!"

Her dad brought the truck to a stop in the middle of the road. There was no shoulder to pull over to, but there was also no other traffic they'd be blocking. Billie threw the door open and ran toward the stream that flowed along one side of the road, stripping her clothes off as she went. By the time she reached the water, she was a bobcat. Shifting always gave her a sense of freedom, a relief from all of the burdens of the human world. She'd never felt that so keenly as she did now, peering down at the water, seeing her own cat face look back at her from the rippling reflection. She ran a few paces, turned in a circle, chasing her own bobtail. Territory *wasn't* an issue, then. But why could she shift here, and not at the house?

Back in human form, she collected her clothes and got dressed as quickly as she could. Her dad was leaning against the truck, conspicuously turned the other way, as though she'd gone out into the forest to pee.

"I couldn't shift back at the house," she explained.

"Nerves?" he asked.

She shook her head. "I'm not sure. Sometimes..." She remembered almost losing her bobcat form in front of the hunters who had treed her back in Juniper. "I guess sometimes my instincts decide I'm safer in human form. Whatever happened back there, it's not a safe place to be a shifter. At least anymore."

Her dad frowned and got back into the truck. Billie slowly slid into her seat, shutting the door behind her.

"I suppose we'll go into town now," he said. "See if anyone can tell us what happened."

The road into Durango was a four-lane highway. The Animas River flowed along one side, and big box stores and franchises lined the other. The highway was so packed with cars that it was difficult to switch lanes, and Billie's dad nearly missed the exit. He navigated through several narrow, busy streets, then parallel parked in one of the few spots available, nearly colliding with a bicyclist as he maneuvered the truck along the curb.

Billie stepped out into the historical downtown. The buildings were mostly brick, a mix of shops and restaurants, hotels and dispensaries, their windows papered in advertisements. Young people drank craft beer on the patios of local breweries. Families carried full bags out of a t-shirt shop. Trashcans overflowed with plastic coffee cups. People sported cameras around their necks or hiking packs slung over their shoulders. Parked cars clogged both sides of the street.

This is what Robyn wants Juniper to be, Billie thought.

They waited at a stoplight for the Walk sign to appear. A woman in a t-shirt promoting an east-coast sports team apparently misinterpreted Billie's goggling at her surroundings and said to her, "Don't you love how quaint this place is?" Billie blinked at her, but the woman was halfway across the street before Billie even noticed the signal had changed, saving her from having to answer. Sure, to someone from a big city, this probably was a quaint, small town. But all she'd ever known was Juniper, and here, she was overwhelmed by the number of cars and strangers, by all the signs and logos, by the distance she'd have to run to get out of the city and back into the forest.

"You okay?" her dad asked as they crossed the road.

She nodded sharply, noticing that her breathing had become a little too rapid.

"What's the plan?" she asked.

He pointed toward the four-story hotel in front of them, a looming red building with ornate white trim. *Great,* Billie thought. *I finally escaped the Silver Coin, and drove six hours to go to Durango's equivalent.* The plan, apparently, was to go out drinking, since her dad passed right by the main hotel entrance and went straight for a door that said "Saloon" over it. This bar was triple the size of the Silver Coin's. An upright piano was tucked against one wall, and a small balcony extended the available seating area. The servers bustling back and forth between the bar and the tables wore Old West saloon girl costumes, complete with corset, fishnet stockings, and oversized feather plumes.

Billie snorted. "Don't ever let Mitch see this place."

Billie's dad leaned across the bar top and asked, "Is Lisa in?"

Before the bartender could answer, a woman's voice projected across the room: "Keith Blackwater. How dare you show your face back in here?"

But there was a playful lilt to the words, no venom. Billie looked up to see a woman in her late forties leaning over the railing of the balcony. Her ample bosom was pushed up and on display in a fringed red showgirl dress and her face was painted with bright red lipstick and thick eyeliner. She turned and disappeared for a moment, before emerging from a staircase onto the main floor, smiling.

"Hello, darling." She gave Billie's dad a lingering kiss on the cheek. "Why didn't you tell me you were coming back to town?"

"What's wrong with a little surprise?"

Billie glanced suspiciously between them. There was something a little too familiar about their body language, a little too playful about their words. Billie's chest began to tighten.

He turned to Billie and opened his arms expansively, encouraging her to step forward to be introduced.

"Lisa, this is my daughter, Billie."

The woman's face lit up in delight and she reached forward and placed her hands on Billie's cheeks. Billie jerked away from the unwanted touch, heart pounding. The woman was crooning about how she'd heard *so much* about her, and how beautiful she'd grown up to be.

"Yeah," Billie said. "I'm his daughter. Who the hell are you?"

Lisa and Billie's dad glanced at each other, and then Lisa said, "Oh, honey, I'm just a friend of your daddy's, that all."

"Friend." Yeah, right. How *dare* he? Her mother was dead by his own hand, and here he was hooking up with some… some…

The woman slid her hands down to Billie's arms now. Billie stepped out of reach. "Don't touch me!" She rubbed her own hands across her arms, smoothing the goosebumps as well as the slight ripple that preceded a shift. Her nervous system was confused and on edge. She shot a glare at her dad and then stormed out of the bar.

He called after her but didn't follow. Billie walked around the corner and leaned heavily against the brick wall. *How could he?*

A logical part of her brain tried to argue that it had been so many years. That despite being dressed like an Old West madame, this Lisa was probably a lovely woman. That her dad was an adult and could have whatever relationships he wanted.

The emotional part of her brain could not care less about any of that. The whole situation just felt wrong. A betrayal. Her mother had loved him, trusted him. And she was dead, because of him, accident or not. Whatever penance he'd done in prison wasn't enough. Why should he be allowed any pleasure?

She'd thought that she'd found a tenuous forgiveness for her dad, but now that had been unraveled all over again. Did Lisa know what he'd done? What kind of woman would want to be with a man who had killed his own wife? Billie was going to walk back in there and make sure she knew everything.

She opened the door and passed through the kitschy bar again.

Lisa was nowhere in sight, but her dad sat at a table alone, two plates of burgers and fries in front of him. He chewed a bite, and lifted a hand to wave Billie over. He gestured to the food.

"Knew you'd come back in eventually. Thought you might be hungry."

"You didn't *know* that. You don't know what I would do," Billie said.

Yet, she *had* come back in. And she *was* hungry. She reluctantly sank into the seat and picked up a french fry.

"Where's Lisa?" Billie tried to pack the name with as much disdain as she could.

"Working," her dad said, without missing a beat.

She passed by then with a tray of food, giving Billie a friendly wink.

"Could have told me you had a girlfriend down here," Billie said.

Her dad shrugged. "Could have. Think you'd have been any happier knowing ahead of time?"

Billie took an overly large bite of burger to keep from saying anything she might regret.

Her dad shook his head. "She's not a girlfriend, anyway. Not really. But I thought she might be able to tell us what happened to the Lesniks."

"The Lesniks?" Billie was confused for a moment. "Oh! The..." The shifter family. "And?"

He chewed, tossed the rest of the burger down on the plate and cleaned his fingers on a napkin.

"Says she hasn't heard from or seen any of them for a couple of weeks. Except for one."

"Stan?" It was the only name Billie could recall, the one her dad had talked about the most.

Her dad shook his head. "Kaitlyn. One of the daughters. Apparently she's a professor at the local college." He held up a clean napkin with a phone number written on it in curly handwriting.

"There's a college here?"

"Not a big one, but yeah."

"So what are we doing dicking around here?" Billie asked.

Her dad shrugged. "Gotta eat. Besides, the person who has the phone took off in a snit."

Billie pulled the phone out of her pocket and tossed it across the table. Her dad ate another french fry, and then picked up the phone.

"Kaitlyn's a… she's like me?" Billie asked.

Her dad frowned. "If she's the one I remember, then no. Not everyone in the family could."

"Oh."

He dialed the number, and cupped one hand over his ear to block out the bar noise.

After a moment, he flipped the phone closed and shook his head. "Answering machine says she's got office hours at the college tomorrow. We can go in and talk to her then, in person."

Billie wanted to protest, but the truth was that she was exhausted, and hungrier than she realized, and overwhelmed by all the newness of this unfamiliar town. So she just nodded and focused on devouring the burger.

"So. Lisa have a spare room for me?"

Her dad shook his head. "Nah. She lives out in Mancos anyway. If it were just me, I'd sleep in the truck."

"Yeah, well, it's not just you," Billie said irritably. They'd been counting on being able to crash at the Lesniks' place and hadn't planned for lodging. "This place is a hotel, isn't it?" She motioned toward the floors above them.

He nodded. "Yeah, but crazy tourist prices. We'll find a cheaper place. At least for the night."

"And after that?"

"One day at a time, baby doll. First we find out if Kaitlyn Lesnik knows what the hell happened to her family."

MONDAY

Billie stared at the motel ceiling, unable to sleep. From the second queen bed across the room, her dad snored, a long, bubbly snonk followed by a whistling exhale. She remembered that snore. When she was a kid, he would frequently pass out on the couch in front of the television. This type of snore was often a cue for her mother to come get her and say it was time to run out into the woods and shift.

They occasionally shifted during the day as well, while he was at work, but it was generally safer at night and they could see so much more. The forest teemed with nocturnal wildlife, and cat eyes used the moonlight like a silver flashlight. Those nights with her mother, roving the forest as a mountain lion and a bobcat, had been the happiest times of Billie's life.

Billie hugged a pillow, trying to let go of the tension in her upper body, but it continued to build. Why hadn't her mom been brave enough to tell her dad their secret? Why did it have to be secret at all? Why did the world refuse to acknowledge that people like her existed?

These were old questions, and they resurged now in the shadows of the motel room, but the real question was what had happened to the Durango shifters? Billie had wondered for years if she might be the only shifter left in the world, until her dad had promised her this whole group. Now, they were gone too. She knew it wasn't actually his fault, but if they really were gone, she wouldn't be able to help but associate that absence with him, blame him for the loss of even more of her family—whether they truly were or not. She'd trusted him, and if his promises proved empty, she didn't think she could ever trust him again.

Deep into the night, her mind spiraled through these worries, along with flashes of memories: climbing trees in human form with her dad down below spurring her on; climbing trees in cat form with her mom alongside her; the taste of her dad's grilled hamburgers, and the smell of his favorite whiskey; the birthday party where no one had shown up and the three of them had beaten the piñata to smithereens together.

In the morning, her dad brought some muffins and hardboiled eggs back from the motel's continental breakfast. As they ate, he said, "Hope my snoring didn't keep you up last night."

"Nah," she lied. "Barely even noticed it."

It was Caleb's first day back at work at the quarry. His leg still ached, but the deep scratches from the Scarlet Monster's claws had scabbed over, and he couldn't really afford much more time off. At least Brock's injury had been on the job, so he was still out, living off of worker's comp checks. It felt weird for Caleb to drive up to the quarry by himself; he and Brock normally carpooled.

The other guys welcomed him back to the quarry in typical male bonding style: high fives and insults and punches in the arm. Caleb struggled through the morning, and by lunchtime, his leg throbbed. He sat on the tailgate of Joaquin's truck and unwrapped the sandwich he'd slapped together that morning, which was already somehow both soggy and stale. He unscrewed the lid of his Nalgene bottle and swallowed another pill with a gulp of warm water.

Joaquin hopped onto the tailgate next to him, making the shocks bounce. "Heard your girl left you."

He should have known people in this bullshit small town would be talking about Billie's trip. If Robyn knew, then everyone would know.

"Nah," Caleb said, mouth full. He swallowed. "No, it's not like that. She's just out of town for a couple of days."

Joaquin and one of the other guys elbowed each other. "Yeah, sure, man," Joaquin said. "I'm just saying, I'd check that bitch for fleas before I let her sleep in my bed again."

He tried to think up some snarky response to Joaquin, but all he could think about was how much his damn leg hurt. "Fuck off," was all he could manage to mutter. Joaquin was just being an asshole, but he was poking at something that had been bugging Caleb since Billie announced her plan to go down to Durango. He'd never been jealous of her here in Juniper—he'd been the one fucking around on her when he was down in Boulder, after all, whereas she wouldn't even shake hands with another guy if she could help it. But now she was away from Juniper, meeting new people. People who were like her. People she was likely to be getting naked and running around the forest with. But they were her cousins, probably, right? Caleb swallowed a chunk of his awful sandwich, and tried to swallow the awful images that kept rising in his mind.

He pulled out his phone and sent Billie a text. Just an innocent enough, "How's it going?" Nothing jealous, nothing possessive. She still hadn't responded to his last text, when he'd told her that Robyn had stopped by with the house papers.

"What the shit is that?" Joaquin said, his burrito falling out of his hand, gaze focused on the forest behind the truck they sat on.

Caleb turned, scanning the forest.

"What the hell," one of the other guys said, and suddenly everyone was on their feet, backing away from something Caleb still couldn't see. He had just about decided this was some kind of hazing joke they were all in on for his first day back, when something suddenly landed on the truck bed behind him with a thump.

It was a squirrel, but its eyes were bright, demonic red, its gray fur ragged and falling off. Like it had mange, or like it had been partially run over and barely survived. The squirrel stood upright on hind legs that looked longer and more muscled than usual for a squirrel. It sniffed at the air. Caleb stared at the creature, dumbfounded, still holding the last bite of his sandwich halfway to his mouth. The squirrel lunged and Caleb dove out of the way. But it wasn't going for him.

"Ah, what the shit?!" Joaquin shrieked, shaking his arm. The squirrel dangled from his forearm by its teeth. He managed to fling it off, but the creature lunged again, emitting a strange, whining cry that sounded nothing like squirrel chatter at all. Joaquin dodged and the squirrel dropped to all fours, tail twitching, poised to pounce again. One of the other guys raced forward, wielding one of the sledgehammers they used to break up big rocks. He swung the sledgehammer like a golf club. The squirrel went flying, smacking into a tree at the edge of the parking lot.

Joaquin shook his arm. Drops of blood welled up from the bite marks. One hand held to his throbbing leg, Caleb limped over to investigate the animal, now nothing but a bloody mess at the base of the tree, hardly identifiable as a squirrel, or anything else.

"Shit, now Joaquin's gonna turn into a were-squirrel," someone said, but no one laughed at the joke.

"Rabies?" someone speculated.

"I never seen rabies look quite like that."

"That's some straight-up Pet Sematary shit," someone said, and kicked dirt over the unmoving squirrel.

But there was only one thing that Caleb knew of that could transform a creature into something demonic and bloodthirsty like that.

"Hey, Joaquin," he shouted. "When's the last time you took Scarlet?"

"The fuck are you, my mom?" Joaquin stalked off, muttering about finding a First Aid kit.

Caleb tried to squat next to the dead squirrel, but winced from the fresh pain that shot through his leg. At the Fourth of July party a couple of weeks ago, he'd taken a vial of Scarlet away from Joaquin, and that's why the monster had gone after Caleb then. It was no surprise that Joaquin was still taking the drug. But the better question was: how had the squirrel gotten a hold of it?

The college in Durango was an old refurbished military base on top of a hill. Her dad drove up the winding road that led up to it, and they parked in a large surface lot. Neither Billie nor her dad had ever been to college, so neither of them knew how to find a professor at one. Billie started to text Caleb to ask, but the question was too long and she kept messing up the letters. She flipped her phone closed and shoved it into her pocket in frustration.

"I don't know, we'll figure it out," she told her dad.

They wandered the campus, reading signs, gradually deciphering what each building was. A digital screen outside of the student union announced intersession hours. Aside from a few people who sat out on the grassy quad or carried boxes between buildings, it was practically a ghost town. A very well-maintained ghost town, with trimmed grass and public art.

Eventually, they identified the chemistry building, and a directory inside listed Dr. Kaitlyn Lesnik's office.

"Can we just walk in there?" Billie's dad asked.

"I dunno." They walked toward the office anyway. Lisa—Billie still felt a bit of spite at her name—had told them Professor Lesnick would likely be in her office even though school wasn't in session.

"That lady is a workaholic," she'd said. "Told me once that she got her so-called *real work* done whenever there weren't students around."

The office door was cracked open, and Billie gave it a tentative knock. A woman's voice invited them in.

She was younger than Billie had expected, mid-thirties, probably. Billie had heard the term "professor" and instantly pictured a bespectacled crone in cat's eye glasses and a tweed skirt suit with a messy gray bun. Kaitlyn Lesnik did have the messy bun, but it was dark brown, and she wore jeans and a loose cotton t-shirt with the periodic table printed across the front. The walls of her office were bare, but the shelves and desk were stacked with a dozen chaotic piles of books and papers.

"Can I help you?" She shut the book she had been looking at and shoved it into a desk drawer. Billie tried to catch a glimpse of the title, something incomprehensible about biochemistry and genetics. She looked to her dad to prompt him to take the lead.

He cleared his throat and extended a hand. "I don't know if you remember me—I met you out at your parents' house? Keith Blackwater."

She scrutinized him for a moment, then gave an overly polite, "Yes, of course, Mr. Blackwater!" and returned the handshake.

"This is my daughter, Billie."

Professor Lesnik extended the handshake to Billie now, and Billie hesitated before reaching out to clasp the other woman's hand. Touch made Billie uncomfortable; Caleb was the only exception. Even something as innocuous as a handshake sometimes felt threatening, a violation of her personal space, a step too close to revealing the secret beneath her skin. But she'd discovered that it was usually too awkward to turn a handshake down, and she could get over her discomfort in a few minutes. Besides, she didn't need to keep her secret from this woman.

Billie gave a perfunctory shake and pulled her hand back as

quickly as she could.

"We stopped by your parents' place earlier," her dad was saying, "but no one was there."

Professor Lesnik adjusted some papers on her desk. "Oh? I'm sure they were simply out. Might have gone camping for a few days."

"I don't think so. It looked… abandoned."

"I'm sorry, are you…" She raised a skeptical eyebrow, scrutinizing both Billie and her dad. "…police officers? Social workers?"

"No, no, nothing like that," Billie's dad said. "We were just coming for a visit. When's the last time you saw them?"

"Mmm, I'm not sure. I've been caught up in my research. Not long, though. I'm sure everything's fine. You have their phone number, I assume?" Professor Lesnik asked.

"Yes, but…"

"Ah," she said, snapping her fingers. "Actually, my mother recently got a new one. Here."

She wrote a number on a sticky note and held it out to him. "Give her a call, I'm sure they'll be back soon and happy to have you over for dinner. But if there's nothing else I can help you with, I have a deadline approaching." She motioned toward the mess of papers on her desk.

Billie's dad opened his mouth to say something, then stopped and dipped his head. "Of course, ma'am. Sorry to bother you."

He started toward the door, but Billie hesitated.

"Since you're into chemistry," Billie found herself saying, mostly just to delay their exit a moment longer, "There's a new street drug called Scarlet. Do you know what it's made from?"

Professor Lesnik cocked her head at Billie and gave her an inscrutable look. "I can't say I've ever heard of it. Maybe the criminology department could tell you more than I could."

"There… haven't been any incidents with it here in Durango?"

"I don't exactly run in those circles, dear, but maybe I'll hear some mention of it from my students. Thanks for the warning."

She wanted to ask more, but Professor Lesnik stood and gestured toward the door. Billie considered telling the woman that she was a shifter too. Maybe that would change the defensive stance she'd taken toward them. But trust went both ways, and Billie wasn't sure she was quite ready to let that information slip. Her dad reached for Billie's arm to guide her out, so Billie turned, keeping a step ahead and out of his reach, and followed him out the office door.

"Well, that was a bust," he said once they were outside the building. "Why'd you ask about Scarlet? You think they were using?"

If the shifters had been taking Scarlet, and one of them had transformed into a monster like Daniel had, there would have been bodies, blood. The Lesnick's house looked like they'd left in a hurry, but there had been nothing like that. It didn't make any sense.

Billie shook her head. "No. Just trying to keep her talking a little longer."

"Yeah, not the friendly type, was she?" He held up the sticky note with the number on it. "Want to let me use your phone?"

Billie handed it to him, and wandered over toward a flyer board on the side of the building while he made the call. Amidst promotions for test prep courses and local band gigs, one flyer advertised Durango Ghost Tours. A cartoonish white ghost stuck its head out of the center of the "O" in "Ghost" in imitation of the *Ghostbusters* logo. Billie reached up and tugged the flyer free of the pin, leaving a little tear at the top of the paper. The ghost she'd talked to back at the Silver Coin had recognized that she was a shapeshifter. He'd said he could tell there was something different about her, and had known others like her before. So it stood to reason if there were ghosts hanging around Durango, they would know about the Lesnik family and might be able to tell her at least when they'd last been around. That was more than they were getting from the living residents of Durango so far.

"Dead number," he said, handing her the phone.

Billie wasn't surprised, but it still irritated her. "Why would she lie to us?"

"Probably she was just trying to get rid of us. I only met her once, before."

Billie showed the flyer to her dad, explained her idea as they walked back toward the parking lot.

"I don't know," he said, skepticism clear. "I think we should just head home."

"If we leave now, we might never find out what happened to them."

"Probably not," he said. "And I am sorry for that."

"You promised me."

"And if I had any damn control over it, I would have delivered on this promise. Maybe if you hadn't pushed me away for so long, we could have gotten down here before anything bad happened to them."

They let that sit between them for a while, neither of them saying a thing. Then, her dad cleared his throat and said, a little more calmly, "Stan said it was dangerous for others to know about who they were, that too many people already knew. I'm betting some of the wrong people found out and thought they would rid the world of some abominations."

Billie narrowed her eyes at him. "That's what you think I am?"

"That's not what I said. Look, Billie, let's just go back to Juniper."

"I'm not ready to give up on this!"

"There's hardly even anything to give up on! You have a lot of extra money to waste on motels?"

He knew damn well she didn't. Billie had a little bit of extra cash that Mitch had given her out of Toby's drug money, back when he thought she'd been the one who killed him. But it wouldn't last long in an overpriced tourist town. Billie bit her tongue. Then, as calmly as she could muster, she said, "One more night."

They stood in front of the truck, her dad swinging the keyring around his finger in a nervous tic.

"What do you think you're going to find?"

"I don't know. Maybe nothing. But I just think, we came all this way, we should at least see the town. I've never been here before. I don't want all this weirdness to be my only memory of our trip, you know?"

He softened somewhat at that.

"Just one more night," she continued. "Since we're here anyway, let's play tourist, see what there is to see. Maybe we'll find out something about the Lesniks, but if not, it can be some quality time. Like we've missed out on for so many years." She raised the flyer again. "You're not afraid of a few ghosts, are you?"

He started to say something, then walked around to the driver's side door and opened it. "Okay, baby doll. One more night."

That was a hell of a first day back, Caleb thought as he pulled up in front of the cabin. He was ready for a long shower and another pain pill and too much beer. He dragged himself inside, but before he could manage any of that, there was another knock on the cabin door.

"Robyn, I swear," Caleb growled as he yanked it open, but it was a different woman who stood on the porch. Pretty, with strawberry blonde hair in a carefully styled curl, soft pink lips and a wide, round face. She wore a flower-print top with flowy sleeves, faded jeans, and flip-flops with rhinestones on the straps.

"Uh, hi," Caleb said, suddenly hyper aware of the sweat stains on his shirt, the uneven stubble on his face.

The woman smiled, a genuinely bright and friendly expression that made her eyes sparkle. "Hi! Sorry, is Billie here?"

Caleb grunted. Yet another person looking for his wayward girlfriend. "Not right now."

"Oh. Well, I'm sorry to bother you. We're moving into town, and

Billie's one of the only people I've made friends with so far." She thumbed over her shoulder at a man leaning against a U-Haul, swiping at his phone in a motion Caleb recognized meant he was catching Pokémon. "That's Luke. I'm Chloe."

"Caleb Mulligan." Caleb extended his hand. Chloe's grip was firm, but her skin was incredibly soft. He let go of her hand before he lingered too long.

"Oh! Related to Mitch Mulligan at the Silver Coin?" she asked.

"Unfortunately." Caleb didn't elaborate.

"Ah. He's been nice enough to us, but I can see how he could be kind of a hard ass. So, anyway, like I said, we're moving in, and I wondered if you might know anyone who could help us carry some furniture? We can pay in beer and pizza, or whatever."

Caleb glanced at the U-Haul. It was one of the smaller trucks that had an attic over the cab. With a couple of strong bodies it shouldn't take very long at all to unload. "Yeah," he said. "I think I can round up some guys to help you."

He got the location from her, and she wrote down her phone number too, with a little smiley face next to it.

"Tell Billie I still owe her a lunch!" Chloe said and waved as she sauntered back toward the U-Haul.

"Sure," Caleb said, confused. Chloe didn't seem like the type of girl Billie would easily befriend, and he didn't remember her mentioning Chloe. More secrets, then.

After he showered and changed clothes, Caleb convinced Joaquin and another guy named Anthony to come with him. He picked them both up and drove up to Chloe's house. With his injury, Caleb had no business helping anyone move. If he kept pushing his leg the way he had that day, it wasn't going to heal properly. The pain pills only dulled it to an aching discomfort rather than a screaming throb, and they made him groggy too. Sluggish, like he was always looking through a fog. He tried to tell himself that he was just being a good neighbor, helping out because it was the nice thing to do. But he recognized the truth was that if Chloe's husband had been the one who'd knocked on his door for help, he wouldn't be on his way over to Snowshoe Drive right now.

The U-Haul was parked in the driveway next to a blue Subaru. Chloe was digging something out of the Subaru's backseat as Caleb pulled the car up. She backed out holding a box against one hip, giving them a wave with her free hand. Joaquin let out a long, low whistle. Chloe's husband stepped down from the U-Haul, chubby and pale, in shorts, sandals, and a Broncos jersey.

"That dweeb scored *her*?" Anthony said from the backseat. "Respect."

Caleb parked behind the U-Haul and they all piled out. Handshakes and introductions all around, and then Chloe started directing which piece of furniture should go where. They got to work, lifting and dragging, sweating and huffing.

"Ooh, careful with that one," Chloe said as Caleb carried a box marked "Shrine" into the house. He set it gently on the coffee table, and Chloe handed him a glass of water. He gratefully plopped down on the still plastic-wrapped couch, and drank most of the water in one long gulp. She pulled up the tape on the box. He swallowed the last of the water and pressed the cool glass against his cheek. She unwrapped small statues and crystals from the box and arranged them on a stand beneath the window.

"Are you, like, a witch?" Caleb asked. That might explain why Billie knew her. Despite what people in town said, Billie was *not* actually a witch, but still, he figured people of various supernatural tendencies might gravitate toward one another.

Chloe glanced at him, a hint of annoyance in the twist of her lips. "Let's just say I'm in touch with the energies of the universe."

"Cool," Caleb said.

"You don't believe me."

Caleb clinked the empty glass onto the coffee table and leaned back. His leg hurt so much he could almost see the pain like a flashing light.

"Hey, if crystals and candles help you make sense of this screwed up world, more power to you." He thought he should probably warn her about the pushback she might get from some of the town's more conservative residents, especially with Reverend Provine's current belief that a devil had been terrorizing the area. But with his leg on fire like this he could hardly form a coherent thought.

"I'm a healer." She unwrapped another statue, kissed it on the head and set it on the altar.

"Yeah?" Caleb said. "Can you heal my leg?"

He said it facetiously, but she cocked her head at him. "Maybe. What did you do to it?"

"Uh…" Caleb tried to figure out how to formulate that answer, but before he could, Chloe's eyes went wide.

"Oh! You were the one who got attacked by that… whatever that was."

"Yeah," Caleb sighed.

She raised her eyebrow at him. "And yet you don't believe in the supernatural."

"I never said I didn't."

Chloe picked up a crystal from the half-constructed altar, held it up to her forehead, and muttered some kind of incantation. Caleb was pretty sure it was only a reflection of light on the window, but the rock seemed to *glow* for a brief moment. She placed it back on the altar, then picked up another one and brought it with her, setting it on the coffee table. She knelt in front of him. Caleb moved his hand away from where he'd been unconsciously clutching his leg, and Chloe slid her hands along his thigh, her eyes closed.

"Ah, there it is," she said as she settled over the spot that throbbed the worst. "It would work better on bare skin, but I think I can work with this."

"Ha," Caleb said awkwardly. Even through the pain, he felt a stirring in his groin. Seeing a gorgeous woman kneeling on the floor in front of him, leaning over his lap, was not helping that growing sensation. Not at all. He shifted his weight a bit, adjusting his jeans.

"Relax," she whispered.

He tried, but there were about a dozen obstacles to that goal, including the fact that someone else could walk in at any second and misinterpret what was happening.

"I should really get back out there to help," he said, but even as he spoke, a calmness washed over him. He closed his eyes and leaned his head back on the couch, the shipping plastic it was still wrapped in squeaking where his head landed.

His leg twinged with a sudden surge of pain, and Chloe gasped at the same time he did. And then, gradually, the pain began to fade. Back down to the tolerable ache that the painkillers took him to, and then, inexplicably, it kept fading more. The muscle unclenched, relaxation washing over his whole leg, relief through his entire body.

The pain was gone. Caleb opened his eyes and looked down, half expecting to see some magical tendrils flowing around his leg. There wasn't anything like that, just Chloe with her eyes closed, forehead bunched in concentration. She kept her hands on his leg for another moment before opening her eyes. She gave his thigh an affectionate squeeze and let go, sitting back on her heels.

"It feels better," he said, incredulous.

Chloe smiled, but it was tight, as though she were the one in pain now. She picked up the pink crystal from the coffee table and held it between her palms. Caleb stayed very still, watching her as she clutched the crystal, her eyes closed. His leg *did* feel better, but he was afraid that as soon as he moved or stood, it would all come rushing back in.

After a moment, Chloe let out a sigh. She stood and carried the pink crystal across the room, but instead of placing it back on the half-constructed altar, she set it in the windowsill. It sparkled in the sunlight.

Caleb heard someone on their way in the door with another load.

He gently moved his leg side to side. Still felt good, free of the gripping pain that had seemed so inescapable a few minutes before. He pushed himself to the edge of the couch, squeaking awkwardly on the plastic covering, and used his arms to push himself up to standing. Anthony and Luke passed by carrying a queen-sized mattress.

Tentatively, he placed weight into the injured leg. Only a tinge of pain, a shadow of what it had been before, like a warning not to push too far. But even that eased a bit as he took a few steps away from the couch.

"I'll be damned," he muttered.

But just as he was about to ask her what had just happened, Joaquin shouted from outside. Caleb hurried toward the propped-open kitchen door. Joaquin stood inside the U-Haul trailer, pointing to an animal in the driveway.

"Dude, what the fuck?" Joaquin yelled again. A yearling buck slowly approached. It had stubby antlers still covered in velvet, but half of the skin on the left side of its face had been torn off, leaving its teeth exposed. The buck was thin enough that ribs showed through its skin, yet its front legs looked bulky and more muscled than a deer had any right to be. Patches of fur were missing, the skin beneath an angry, inflamed red.

Anthony and Chloe came up behind Caleb. He put an arm out, trying to block them from going outside. Joaquin was still in the back of the U-Haul, not moving, just watching the animal. It was watching him, too, stepping slowly forward, head low, moving like a cat stalking a mouse. And then it charged, leaping off the ground into the U-Haul. Joaquin dove out of its way. The deer crashed into some of the remaining boxes. While it struggled to find its footing again, Joaquin yanked the roll up door down and slammed the latch into place, trapping the creature inside.

"It's the devil," Anthony said. "Just like Reverend Provine said."

"It's not the devil," Caleb said. He let go of the doorframe and jumped over the flattened cardboard boxes they'd placed over the steps to create a ramp for the dolly. His leg twanged in warning on the landing, but it didn't buckle and the pain didn't rush back in.

The U-Haul rocked violently as the creature slammed against the walls from inside.

Anthony and Chloe followed Caleb hesitantly out into the driveway. Luke appeared a moment later, saying, "Hey, honey, which drawer did you want the silverware in?" He looked up in alarm as the U-Haul rocked again.

"You got a gun?" Joaquin shouted to Luke.

"Huh?" Luke said.

"Look at him," Anthony said. "Of course he don't have a gun."

Caleb looked to Chloe, and she shook her head.

"Shit!" Joaquin shouted, throwing his arms up at the sky.

"What is it, a bear?" Luke asked.

"It's the fucking devil in there," Anthony declared again, almost reverently.

"It's not the devil," Caleb repeated. "It's like that squirrel."

"What squirrel?" Chloe asked.

"It's a squirrel trapped in there?" Luke asked, confused.

Caleb gave an irritated sigh and walked over to grab Joaquin by the arm.

"You have Scarlet on you?"

"What?"

"Scarlet, asshole. You've been dosing?"

"A drop or two here and there. Takes the edge off. Maybe you should try some and mind your own damn business."

The U-Haul rocked again, and an uncanny scream echoed from inside. Suddenly everyone was shouting, yelling at each other. Anthony had dropped to his knees and started praying.

"Okay, can everyone shut the hell up for a minute?" Caleb yelled over the noise.

All eyes turned back on him.

"At high doses," he explained. "Scarlet transforms people—or whatever, I guess—into literal monsters that go after everyone else who has the drug in their bloodstream. That devil-looking thing that attacked me on Fourth of July was *not* an actual devil, it was a person who had overdosed on Scarlet."

"The deer's... on drugs?" Chloe asked. Everyone was frowning, trying to make sense of what he'd said.

"Goes after everyone who has it in their..." Joaquin mumbled, then looked up sharply at Caleb. "Then you were taking it, too? Hypocrite."

"No," Caleb said, exasperated. "Remember, I took that vial from you. I had it in my pocket. That's why it came after me. Otherwise, it definitely would have targeted you." *And you'd definitely be dead right now, you ungrateful bastard.* Caleb rubbed his leg where the monster had attacked him, still amazed that it didn't hurt anymore.

"Oh, yeah. I forgot you stole that shit from me. What the hell did you do with it?"

"The vial fell... Oh, god." As the Scarlet Monster had carried him across the lake, Caleb had dropped the Scarlet vial into the lake, thinking the creature might dive after it and let him go. But it had carried him all the way to an abandoned building before realizing that Caleb didn't have the drug anymore. "It fell into the lake," Caleb said. "Where the animals drink from."

"But even if it infected the water, it would be diluted, wouldn't it?" Chloe asked. "I mean, how strong is this stuff?"

"I don't know," Caleb said. Maybe the vial had washed up on shore before it broke, or ended up in a shallow pool along the edge of the lake, like the one he'd seen that deer drinking from the other day. Maybe even this same deer. There must have been enough Scarlet in the water to affect at least two animals, in any case.

The creature slammed against the inside of the truck again, this time leaving an indent.

"Give me your keys," Joaquin said to Caleb. "I'm going to get my

Remington."

"Not sure we have time for that," Caleb said as the rollup door rattled and bent with another hit.

"Could we tranquilize it?" Chloe said, and everyone turned to look at her. "I have sleeping pills."

They all looked at each other for a moment, and then Caleb realized they were all waiting on him to give the yes or no. He shrugged. "We could try."

He followed Chloe inside. She dug in a box in the bathroom and pulled out a bottle of pills and another of gummies with a moon on the label. She poured some of both out into her hands. "How much, do you think? I don't want to hurt it."

"It wants to hurt *you*, so more is probably better."

Caleb took the pills from her and turned to go back outside.

"If it goes to sleep, maybe I could heal it," she said.

Caleb started to say *no way*. But then he remembered how badly Billie had wanted to save Daniel once she'd recognized he was the one who had been transformed. He was pretty sure if she were here right now, she would want to try to save the deer too rather than just let Joaquin shoot it.

"That thing you did with my leg—you could do that with the deer?"

"I don't know," Chloe said. "But I could try."

Joaquin came inside to see what the hell was taking them so long. "You have any Scarlet on you?" Caleb asked him. He grabbed a plastic bowl out of one of the open boxes in the kitchen.

"No." First time he'd given a straight answer like that, so Caleb believed him.

"Great. Then I need your blood."

"What?"

"You can give it willingly, or I can fucking cut you." Caleb dumped the sleeping pills into the bowl. "If we want it to eat this shit, then we have to use your blood, because that's what it's actually after."

"Jesus Christ," Joaquin said. "When did you get to be such a fucking cult leader?" But he did it. Joaquin took his pocket knife out, pricked his thumb, and bled a few thick drops onto the sleeping pills.

"Stay in here," Caleb told the others, and carried the bowl outside.

The U-Haul was rocking so aggressively that Caleb feared it might fall over onto its side. Luke was out there still, filming the drama on his phone.

"Put that away," Caleb said, "and go inside with the others."

He didn't even wait to see if Luke obeyed his directions. Caleb put a hand on the latch, took a long breath, then yanked the roll up door partway up. He slid the bowl across the floor, and slammed it shut again. The rocking stopped for a moment, and Caleb could hear a snuffling sound. Then the rocking started again, and an antler stabbed through the wall. Caleb backed away and ran back for the kitchen door.

"Did it work?" Joaquin asked.

Caleb shut the screen door behind him, though it felt like a flimsy defense. "I don't know. It'll take some time for the pills to take effect."

How long? Twenty minutes, half an hour? Would it knock itself out before then by battering the walls, or would it smash hard enough that it would manage to break all the way out?

"So, if there's Scarlet in the water," Joaquin said, "and the animals have been drinking it, and turning into—" He waved his hand toward the U-Haul. "—*that*, then what you're really telling me is we're about to have a zombie animal invasion on our hands."

Caleb nodded gravely. "It's a distinct possibility."

Joaquin looked Luke over with a disgusted sneer. "Get yourself a gun. And welcome to the mountains."

The ghost tour didn't start for hours, so Billie and her dad had to find other things to fill the afternoon. For a while, they drove around town, stopping at various shops and construction offices—places that might have been clients of Stan Lesnik's blade-sharpening business—to ask if anyone had seen him or knew where to find him. When that didn't turn up any leads, they really did just play tourist.

Most of the tourist offerings in Durango were things like Jeep tours or ziplining; outdoorsy adventures that were likely more of a novelty to someone not used to mountain living. All the big national monuments like Mesa Verde and Chimney Rock were another hour's drive out of town, and neither Billie nor her dad were particularly interested in historical ruins anyway. They ended up going to a railroad museum, and though they talked about riding the train up to Silverton, tickets cost more than their motel room, so instead they stood on the bridge and watched the train rumble past.

Billie sent Caleb a picture of the train, but although he should have been available at that point in the evening, he didn't respond. She started to type a message, pushing each number until the right letter appeared, but how could she say anything meaningful in this clunky way? She deleted the few letters she'd typed, flipped the phone closed, and shoved it into her pocket, hoping the picture would be enough to let Caleb know she was at least thinking of him.

The ghost tour began at seven, meeting in the lobby of the hotel with the old west saloon, and Billie felt a strange sort of déjà vu. She was glad she wasn't the one telling ghost stories to this much larger group. A man around Billie's age played tour guide, and he had obviously memorized a script. The group slowly worked their way along Main Avenue, listening to his stories about the mines and the brothels, tuberculosis victims and snake oil salesmen. In front of a tavern, the guide described a famous shootout in 1906, over a crackdown on illegal gambling. *Not so different from Juniper at all,* Billie thought. Just a little bigger, and full of strangers.

Most of the actual ghost stories were vague, or sounded like residual hauntings: the laughter of children in a basement, strange faces glimpsed in a mirror, guttural voices on an EVP recording. Back in Juniper, Heather had explained to Billie that residual hauntings were not really a soul trapped on this side of the veil, but more like leftover energy, an imprint in the ether that replayed on a loop. Intelligent hauntings were far more rare, and they tended to hide from people the way a wild animal would. *That* was the elusive type of ghost Billie needed. So far, the tavern ghost seemed the most likely candidate. If he was real, maybe she could spot him, talk to him. She would have to check back in the stillness of the night.

The traffic had nearly disappeared by now, and the group trickled across the street in the middle of a block. As she stepped onto the sidewalk, Billie caught a scent on the wind. She paused, drawing in more air, trying to sort out if she smelled what she thought she did. It was hard to trust her human nose, but this mix of dry red wine and coppery blood sure reminded her of Scarlet. The group flowed around her while she looked around for any indication of where the scent might have come from. Someone in the group? Several of them were sunburned, but none sported the extreme redness and peeling like Daniel or Tara had after they'd taken too much. She looked toward the rooftops. No Scarlet Monsters perched on the awning above them, waiting to attack. The group had stopped at the end of the block, gathered in a half-circle around the guide; Billie hurried to catch up.

"And if you'll note just here where this young lady is standing…"

The guide pointed at Billie and she felt a surge of panic before realizing he was pointing toward something under her feet. She stepped backwards, looking down. She'd been on top of an ancient-looking manhole cover.

"You'll see these unique manholes up and down this block. Underneath—" He stomped his foot a couple of times on the pavement. "—are hollow rooms and tunnels. More than fifteen different Colorado cities have underground tunnels like these. Built around the 1880s, some say the tunnels were a secret passageway that led between bars and brothels. A gentleman could walk into a respectable saloon, meet a lady of ill repute, and follow her through these tunnels to a not-so-respectable brothel a few streets over, so that he wouldn't be seen entering such a place."

The mental image that formed in Billie's mind as the guide told this story was a sepia-tinted Old West scene, with her dad as the "gentleman" and Lisa as the "lady of ill repute."

"Now," the guide continued, "As romantic and interesting as that story is, it isn't quite the truth here in Durango. Our tunnels are more like hollow sidewalks. A century ago, the coal truck would rumble down the street, dumping coal through the manholes so that shopkeepers didn't have to haul it through their stores to reach the furnace. Most of these underground rooms have been blocked off now, but some of the local shops still use them for storage. While we don't have any confirmed ghost sightings in these tunnels, sometimes we hear some very strange, unexplainable sounds on this block." He went on to tell the story of a t-shirt shop employee who had recently reported bizarre noises as well as objects inexplicably moved near the sealed-off door.

As the group shuffled toward their next stop, Billie's dad hung back. He'd been gradually growing restless for the whole tour.

"What is it?" Billie asked, thinking maybe he'd discovered some clue. But he hooked his thumb toward the tavern across the street and said, "I'll catch up with you in a couple of minutes."

Billie frowned, but she didn't protest. He disappeared into the tavern and she followed the tour guide to the next location, and the next. She knew her dad had no intention of catching up. By the time the tour circled back around to the hotel where they'd started, it didn't surprise her that he wasn't there to meet her.

The tour guide thanked them for coming, asked for tips, and the crowd gradually dispersed. Billie waited until almost everyone had wandered off, and then she approached the guide.

"I was wondering," she asked. "If you know the Lesnik family?"

The guide shook his head. "Doesn't sound familiar, sorry."

"Okay," she said. It had been a long shot, but she had no idea who knew who in this unfamiliar place. "Do you know of any other, um, strange sightings around here?"

"You mean like Bigfoot? There was a picture taken up by Silverton a couple of years ago."

Billie resisted the urge to roll her eyes. Why was it always *Bigfoot*? But she listened as he rattled off the story of the blurry photograph in front of the train, and then somehow veered into an ancient aliens theory that claimed a pyramid-shaped mountain to the southwest was a buried mothership.

"The Bigfoot," Billie said. "Could be like a skinwalker, maybe? A shapeshifter?"

She watched his face for any twitch of recognition or suspicion at the word, but he only shrugged. "Guess it could."

Trying to keep her tone neutral, conversational, she asked, "Do you get many animals in town? Regular ones, I mean. Or does the highway mostly keep them out?"

"Sure. Lots of coyotes. Bears, sometimes."

"Bobcats?" Billie asked.

"Never seen one, but I guess they might be around." He pulled a smartphone out of his pocket and glanced at the screen. "Sorry, I've got to head out. Anything else I can help you with?"

Billie took a deep breath and let it out. "Just one, sorry to take up your time. Any chance you know anything about Scarlet?" This type of questioning hadn't gone well with the professor, but she'd *smelled* it this time.

"Is that a strand of weed?" the guide asked.

"No," Billie said. "It's... Nevermind."

He gave her the rundown on his favorite dispensaries in town anyway, and Billie listened politely, then thanked him and broke away.

Billie retraced the path they'd taken on the ghost tour as best she could remember, pausing at each location to watch and listen for any hint of a ghost. But there were still far too many people out. The tavern where her dad had gone for a drink was raucous and busy. With that much activity, there would surely be no hope of glimpsing a ghost. She continued the loop anyway, thinking she might spot some clue she'd missed when following the crowd.

When she caught that faint scent of Scarlet again, she stopped. Maybe it wasn't Scarlet at all. Human senses were terrible at identifying anything but the most obvious and pungent smells. This could be a type of cheap perfume or incense from the tourist shop, or a by-product from the breweries that Billie wasn't used to smelling in Juniper.

With a deep breath, she closed her eyes, trying to shift only enough to sharpen her senses. Smells poured in, and when she opened her eyes, the night was vibrant and alive. Her body remained human, but if anyone had been close enough, they would have seen the yellow slits of cat's eyes, like the boys she'd scared at the Juniper cemetery.

The smells were overwhelming, and harder to process than when she was in full bobcat form. But yes, she was more sure now that the faint scent definitely matched her memory of Scarlet.

If she could shift all the way, she could follow the scent trails, maybe track it to its source. But this wasn't Juniper—she couldn't just go out to her cave, or pop into the abandoned livery stable next to her cabin to shift. Here, she had no idea where she could go that she wouldn't be seen. Was it worth it to try? If she didn't, then tomorrow morning, her dad would drive her back to Juniper, and she'd leave with no answers and even more questions than she had before. She didn't know if Scarlet might have anything to do with the Lesniks' disappearance, but last time someone was missing, the drug had turned out to play a major role. She finished retracing the ghost tour, and then wandered a little past downtown, following the sound of the river.

Even as late as it was, people were out walking dogs, jogging, or sitting on benches along the path. Trees and bushes lined the bank, but nothing dense enough to provide any kind of concealment. Billie considered a dark underpass, until she got closer and saw two homeless people camped. No privacy there, then. Billie zeroed in on a willow tree. Its branches drooped all the way to the ground, creating a skirt: a veil of leaves thick enough she couldn't see through them to the trunk. That might work.

As she approached, a couple of young people pushed aside a branch and stumbled out of the hollow, laughing. Billie waited until they'd crossed the bridge, then went closer to investigate the tree. The low-hanging branches formed something like a cave. It smelled like sex and marijuana. The ground under the branches was littered with cigarette butts and beer cans. But it appeared to be fairly secluded, a spot where kids could secretly rendezvous or sneak a toke while people passed right by without knowing they were there. Or where a shapeshifter could change shape without being seen.

Billie waited inside the pseudo-cave for a little while, making sure that the couple didn't come back, and no one else was going to stop in. Then under the cover of the branches, she took off her clothes and laid them in a pile. She folded herself, landed on four paws. Yes, she was going to stick with bobcat even though the tour guide had said they weren't common in the area. A regular cat would be more convenient, stealthier, but the form was too small. She could manage a dog, but it was uncomfortable, and she'd had trouble holding it in the past. She didn't want to risk snapping out of the form at the wrong moment. Besides, she needed her feline night vision to navigate in the dark. She would slink in the shadows, stay out of sight. Billie peeked out of the bush, and, seeing no one, darted out and back toward Main Avenue.

It was almost impossible to stick to the shadows once she caught the Scarlet scent again, as the scent trail went right down Main Street, where too many street lights made it nearly as bright as day. The scent was difficult to follow in the first place, with the air crisscrossed with the trails of so many people, thick with car exhaust and the pungent aromas from all the restaurants and breweries. Most scent trails were like the chemical footprints of someone or something passing through. This was more like a cloud, permeating the air for an entire block. She sniffed around the manhole cover where the ghost tour guide had stopped earlier, noticing a slight concentration there. But then a shop door opened behind her, and she darted off into the alleyway as quickly as she could. It was too dangerous to be sniffing around in this form in this unfamiliar place. She'd tried, but this venture wasn't giving her any new answers.

On her way back to the river, though, a fresh scent trail stood out. Billie stopped in her tracks, senses sharpened from fear, eyes wide to search for movement in the shadows. Male, starving, and a cloud of Scarlet. It was *so* similar to the scent she'd detected near Toby Moran's house, which had turned out to belong to Daniel Gadbury after he'd taken too much Scarlet and transformed into something demon-like. Billie tracked the scent back to the river, almost to the same area where she'd left her clothes inside the willow tree.

If there was a Scarlet Monster on the loose in Durango, Billie needed to get back to human form. She might be able to fight it better while shifted, but it would be bright red. Feline vision was red-green colorblind, so the red that would be so obvious to her human eyes would blend into the shadows. It was a trade-off. Besides, she didn't *want* to fight a creature like that again, if she didn't have to.

On her way to the willow, a flash of movement made her jump and drew her gaze away from the tree.

A coyote padded through the grassy riverwalk. It stopped and looked directly at her, ears back and tail tucked under. Part of its fur looked like it had been scraped off, bloody and matted. The coyote stared at Billie for a moment longer, then limped off in the direction of the river.

Billie hesitated before following the scent trail directly to where the coyote had just stood. Had the Scarlet scent come from the coyote? But that didn't make any sense. Billie sniffed around the spot for a while, keeping an eye out in case the coyote came back or any other surprises leaped out of the shadows at her. But she couldn't make sense of the scent signature, couldn't parse out whether the Scarlet was part of the coyote's scent or whether it was just clinging to her fur from earlier.

After a while, she stopped circling the spot and went back to the tree where she'd hidden her clothes.

But when she made it back there, Billie found to her dismay that the clothes were strewn out across the grass. Her underwear lay on the sidewalk; her shirt crumpled in the mud at the river bank. The scent signature of a couple of racoons circled the bush and disappeared into a drain culvert.

Really? she thought, suppressing the urge to let out a frustrated caterwaul.

Watching for onlookers, Billie retrieved each piece of clothing with her teeth and dragged them back inside the tree's canopy. Her shirt was streaked with mud, but nothing to be done about that. At least she'd been able to recover everything except for one sock.

In human form and dressed again, Billie peaked out from behind the leaves, searching for any flashes of bright red, any leathery wings or demonic claws. Nothing but some chirping insects and night birds. Billie headed back toward the downtown. She'd gathered a couple of clues, but she wasn't sure they were even part of the same mystery she'd been trying to solve. Red herrings, surely, a waste of time. Maybe in the morning they could take one more trip to the Lesniks' house before they left town, and they'd discover it was all a misunderstanding and the family had merely been out for a long weekend trip, like Kaitlyn had said.

At the bar, her dad was finishing up a game of pool. When his opponent sank the eight ball, he tossed the pool stick onto the table and plopped himself onto a barstool.

"Okay, time to go," Billie told him.

"The night is young, and so are we!" He raised his beer bottle in mock toast and then downed the last of it.

"You're… not that young," Billie said. "And it's late. Come on, let's go."

He slammed the bottle on the table and announced, "Next round's on me!"

Everyone within earshot cheered, but Billie shouted, "No it isn't. He doesn't have money for that." She hoped he hadn't spent the little he had in his wallet all on beer. The cheers turned to boos. He was slouched over the bar now. Billie spotted the truck keys in his back pocket and snaked them out. She held the keys just out of his reach.

"Fine, you stay here all night. I'm going to take the truck back to the motel by myself."

She'd expected him to take the bait, but he acted like he hadn't even heard her.

"Hey, gimme another one," he said to the bartender.

"Nah, buddy," the bartender said. "I think your girl's right. Time to go home."

A flash of anger rippled across his face, and Billie sucked in a quick breath. Her dad had never hurt her—not physically, anyway—but she'd seen him snap with other men, had heard stories of him getting into fights over smaller offenses than this.

She laid a hand on his arm, even though the touch made her practically burn with discomfort. "Dad. Please?"

He looked over at her, and his anger softened, deflated. "Okay," he said. "Okay." He slipped getting off of the barstool and Billie caught him, hauled him to his feet. He staggered out the door, but about half a block from the bar, he collapsed and sprawled on the sidewalk.

"Dad!" She grabbed a fistful of his shirt and shook. "Dad, come on, wake up!"

He groaned and rolled his head from side to side. He lifted an arm to shield his eyes from the streetlight. Billie grabbed that arm and used it to pull him up to sitting.

He mumbled, "Valerie," and Billie paused. That had been her mother's name.

"No, it's me, Dad, it's Billie. We have to get back to the truck."

"I'm sorry, Valerie," he mumbled again.

"She's not here," Billie said. *You killed her,* she didn't say.

He bent one knee and drove a boot heel into the sidewalk. Billie slung his arm around her shoulder and helped him stand. He was healthier now than he had been when he'd first arrived back in Juniper, but he was still very thin, a small-framed man to begin with who had hardly eaten enough for months after he got out of prison. Billie was small too, but she was strong enough to hold him up. The path to the truck was straight and flat, even if it was still a couple of blocks away.

"Come on," she told him. "Let's go this way."

He stumbled along beside her on unsteady legs, occasionally leaning against her too much and almost knocking both of them over.

"I love you, Valerie," he slurred, and this time, Billie didn't bother to say anything back.

"This is why we don't go anywhere," Billie remembered her mom telling him once as she'd guided him into the house and toward the bedroom, supporting him in this same awkward way. It was the weekend before Halloween, and the two of them had gone down to Fred's Bar and Grill on Miners Avenue—the Silver Coin hadn't been revamped yet back then—for a Halloween karaoke contest. *So the grownups can play dress-up, too,* they'd told Billie before they left. Billie was almost eleven, and they'd been trusting her lately to stay alone more and more often.

Billie's mother wore a plastic black cat mask that only covered her eyes. Furry black ears poked up from a headband, and a long string of tinsel pinned to her waistband approximated a tail. Her dad wore a black cape, but his white makeup had streaked and smudged away, and the fake plastic vampire teeth were long gone. His cape was crooked, twisted over one shoulder, vomit stains running down the edges of it.

Billie had pulled her knees up to her chest on the couch as she watched them stumble past. The unsteady way he'd swayed and stepped, as though the floor was moving beneath his feet, had scared Billie more than the horror movie she'd been watching on TV. She'd seen her dad drunk dozens of times over the years, but usually he simply passed out on the couch. This was different. Like he existed on a different plane of geometry than the rest of the world. Like couldn't see what was right in front of him. His boot hit the coffee table, and Billie's mom steered him around it. They disappeared into the bedroom, and Billie could hear him gagging, throwing up. She hugged her knees closer to her chest, turned the volume up to drown out the horrible sounds from the other room with screams and suspenseful music. Fake horrors to hide from the real ones.

After a few minutes, her mom came back out and flopped heavily onto the couch beside her. She took her cat mask off and tossed it onto the coffee table.

"*What* are you watching?" She took the remote and changed the channel away from the horror movie, landing on some inane sitcom. But then she turned the volume all the way down. "You know he'd never hurt you, right? Not the way his dad hurt him. That's why he does things like this, you know. He hurts all the time, and drinking is the only thing that makes that pain go away. So he has too much, because he keeps searching for ways to make it all disappear. Do you understand?"

Billie hadn't understood, not at all. She didn't know what a Halloween party had to do with her grandfather's belt, or how some bitter liquid could make anything better. But she'd nodded, and her mom had hugged her and assured her it was all going to be okay.

But now, stumbling their way to the truck while her dad muttered incoherent sentences, still convinced he was talking to "Valerie," Billie thought she did understand. She didn't agree with it, didn't think it was the best way to cope, didn't appreciate that now she had to be the one to clean him up and take care of him. But, she thought that she finally understood what her mom had been trying to tell her about him, all those years ago.

Once the creature stopped banging against the inside of the U-Haul, Caleb unlatched the roll up door and slowly eased it open a couple of inches. Joaquin stood nearby, wielding a metal baseball bat, the closest thing to a weapon they'd been able to locate in Chloe and Luke's belongings. Despite Caleb's warnings for everyone to wait inside, Anthony, Chloe, and Luke all stood on the back door steps, watching. When nothing reached out of the gap, Caleb rolled the door up a little higher. It got stuck about halfway, too bent and damaged to go any higher.

Joaquin lowered the baseball bat and whistled. "Hope you got the insurance, bro," he said as Luke came closer to inspect the damage, Chloe trailing behind him.

At the sight of the deer, Luke gagged, putting a hand to his mouth. Chloe, to her credit, did not. The creature was collapsed on the floor of the truck, the mangled half of its face on top, a thick purple tongue lolling out of the lower half.

"Is it dead?" Anthony asked. He'd stayed near the back door.

It sure looked dead. Caleb grabbed the support bar and ducked under the door to get a closer look. The deer's ribs rose and fell with the slightest movement.

"It's alive," Caleb declared. He pulled on the work gloves he'd taken out of the car. "Help me get it out of here."

Joaquin tossed down the baseball bat and hopped up into the

truck. Each of them grabbed two of the deer's spindly legs. Its head looked like it was about to fall off its neck as they dragged it out of the U-Haul. Luke peered inside, complaining about all of the things it had destroyed. Caleb and Joaquin hefted the deer over to the edge of the driveway and set it down at the base of a tree. Caleb grabbed a piece of rope that had been used to hold furniture in place. He tied it around the deer's neck and secured the other end to the tree.

"Think that'll hold it?" Joaquin asked skeptically.

"Hoping we don't have to find out," Caleb said. He turned and made eye contact with Chloe, waved her over toward them. "Do you want to try?"

She held her crystals, a couple of bigger ones she'd dug out of the shrine box while they waited. Slowly, she approached the animal and knelt in front of it.

Luke hopped down from the U-Haul and said, "Oh my god, Chloe, don't touch that thing!"

"Shh!" she said. "What did I tell you about interrupting me during a ritual?"

"But…" Luke looked bewildered.

Joaquin and Anthony snickered at him. But then to Caleb, Joaquin said, "The hell is she doing, though?"

"She's a healer," Caleb said. "She's going to try to…" He faltered, then went with, "She's going to try to get the devil out of it."

"Like *The Exorcist*?" Anthony said. "That's badass."

"Shh!" Chloe repeated, to all of them this time.

She placed her hands on the deer's torso, in between the various raw patches. Caleb watched her shoulders rise and fall with long, slow breaths. Everyone else held their breath, waiting for something to happen. Just when they were starting to grow restless, the deer twitched, and Chloe gave a little mewl of pain. She hunched over the animal a moment longer, then suddenly fell backward, as though pushed or flung by an explosive force. All of the guys immediately ran toward her. The deer twitched again, and Joaquin and Luke stopped short.

"Chloe," Caleb said urgently. He grabbed her arms and shook her. Though she lay still, her skin writhed beneath his hands. He let go in surprise. Caleb had only seen Billie shapeshift a couple of times, but her skin rippled in this same way, as though the solidness of her body became liquid. Chloe wasn't a shapeshifter too, was she? It seemed so unlikely. And Billie didn't have any of the healing powers that Chloe had. No, more likely that it was a side effect, somehow, of attempting to heal the deer. He regretted that he hadn't talked her out of it.

Chloe wheezed and flung an arm out, grasping handfuls of dirt like she was reaching for something. She'd dropped the big crystal; it lay on the ground just beyond her fingertips. Caleb leaned over and grabbed it, then placed the stone into her hand. She wheezed again and closed her bloodshot eyes, pulling the crystal to her chest and wrapping her other hand around it as well.

In the background, Caleb heard Luke on the phone saying, "It's my wife, she's having some type of seizure…"

Of course, Luke wouldn't know that it could take up to an hour for an ambulance to navigate the mountain roads, making 911 pretty useless for emergencies in Juniper.

Suddenly, Chloe opened her eyes, less bloodshot now, and sat up with a "Whoo!" of relief. She opened her hands. The crystal she'd been holding had cracked. It was smashed, in fact, into tiny shards.

"She's okay," Caleb shouted to Luke as Chloe brushed the stone shards and pink dust from her hands.

Luke lowered the phone away from his ear and started over toward them. "Okay, never mind, false alarm," he said to the dispatcher and then shoved the phone into his pocket. Chloe reached for Luke, and Caleb moved out of the way. She wrapped her arms around Luke's neck. He scooped her into his arms and carried her inside the house.

"That didn't look like no exorcism," Anthony said nervously.

"Did it work?" Joaquin asked.

Caleb looked at the deer. It was breathing faster now, but certainly didn't look "healed." It was currently debilitated, but Caleb was pretty sure it would wake up mad. "I don't think so."

"Got a plan B?"

Caleb pulled his car keys out of his pocket and shoved them at Joaquin. He took them without comment and jumped into the car. He'd be back in a few minutes with a rifle and a shovel, and they'd cover this whole mess up. But if more animals were drinking Scarlet-infected water, this wouldn't be the last one they'd have to deal with.

Caleb went into the house and found Luke in the kitchen, digging a tea kettle out of a box.

"Sorry you had to see that, man." Luke kept his voice low. "She gets so worked up sometimes. Hysterical. Kind of… delusional. I've tried to get her to see a psychiatrist, but she won't go." He turned on the tap and filled the tea kettle.

Caleb frowned. He just nodded to Luke and kept going, into the living room. Chloe was on the couch now, still with that protective plastic covering over it. He knelt beside her and she reached for his hand.

"Sorry I couldn't save the deer," she said. Her voice was hoarse, almost a whisper.

"You…" Caleb started, still thinking it through. "You take the pain into yourself. Then you transfer it into the stones."

She smiled. "You get it. I think… I think maybe you have some magic in you as well."

"What? No. No way."

She nodded slowly. "You do. I can feel it right now." She squeezed his hand. "I could sense it in you right away. That's why it was so easy for me to heal you."

His other hand went to his leg again. An hour ago, he wouldn't even have been able to kneel down in this position without excruciating pain. There was a little ache in it now, but it was more like a muscle that hadn't been used in a while, a good soreness like after a day at the gym.

Luke came in with the tea then, and Caleb squeezed her hand and then let it go.

"You get some rest," Caleb said. "I'll finish unloading your boxes."

What he could salvage of them, anyway.

Once Billie managed to get her dad to the truck, she reached for her phone to check the time, but the phone wasn't there.

"Shit," she muttered. She reached under the seats, checked the console. No phone anywhere, and she realized where it had probably been left. *Damn racoons.*

"We have to take a detour," she told her dad, but he was slumped against the window, not fully conscious.

She drove back the direction she'd come from and parked across several spaces in the riverwalk's small parking lot. Everyone who had been jogging or walking earlier was gone by now, leaving the area free of people. The streetlights here were too dim and spaced too far apart to see much with her human eyes. She searched the area where she'd retrieved her clothes earlier, and then on a hunch, navigated down a steep slope. Dust billowed around her as her foot slid and she landed on the riverbank.

There was the phone near the water, caked with mud, but perfectly safe. She wiped the mud off, checked the time. It was even later than she'd thought, and her battery was almost dead. There were a couple of messages from Caleb, but she'd have to look at those later. A sudden breeze whipped her hair across her face, and brought with it the scent of Scarlet, so strong it practically made her eyes water. Billie turned in the direction the scent had come from, and yelped in surprise when she saw the shadow of something on the riverbank a little ways down.

Her heart pounded with the adrenaline rush, but the creature didn't move. As her brain started to make sense of the shape, she realized what she was looking at.

"Baby doll, are you okay?" her dad shouted, panic clear in his voice.

"I'm fine, Dad," she shouted back. "It's just a coyote. It surprised me."

The coyote, probably the same one she'd seen earlier, had collapsed on the riverbank. It panted, eyes shut. She could hear her dad's clumsy footsteps as he stumbled out of the truck to look for her. She should probably go before he fell down the slope, and before she got too close to the animal. It was clearly sick.

But just before Billie turned away from the coyote, something started to happen. The body grew larger, the fur receded, the limbs stretched and reformed.

The coyote unfolded and a man remained.

A naked man, laying on his side, blood running from a cut on his head. His ribcage heaved with heavy, labored breaths.

Billie's dad slid down the slope the same way Billie had, creating a cloud of dust as he landed awkwardly at the bottom. He got to his feet and came up behind Billie. She could hardly breathe.

"Thought you said a coyote," he said.

"That's what he was a moment ago," she said, and the implications of that hit them both at the same time.

Her dad was much steadier on his feet now, seemingly sobered by adrenaline. He knelt down and rolled the man over. One arm slung across his body, his head turned sharply to one side. It was so similar to the position her mother had landed in after her dad had shot her, when she'd shifted back to human form and fallen in their backyard, and he'd realized what he'd done. But—she looked the man over—he had no shotgun blast in his chest, and no gunpowder scent lingered in the air. A tangle of dark hair covered his face, and a coyote paw tattoo was stamped on his chest.

"Yeah," her dad said. "That's one of Stan's kids. Trent? Travis? Something like that." He leaned down and put his arms under the man's shoulders, then looked back up at Billie and snapped, "What are you waiting for? Grab his legs."

Billie really didn't want to grab a strange man's legs, but she did, sliding her hands under his calves and lifting. She looked over her shoulder as she walked backward. They found a slightly less steep area of the slope and struggled up it. Her dad hefted him into the truck bed and tossed a tarp over him. Billie had an uncomfortable flashback to when they'd loaded Daniel Gadbury into the back of Mitch's truck. They'd taken him to the hospital, hoping they could save him, transform him back to human from the winged monster the Scarlet had turned him into, but he hadn't made it.

"Does Durango have a hospital?" Billie asked once she and her dad were both back in the truck's cab. Her hand shook as she shifted the truck into gear.

"Let's just take him with us back to the room."

"What?"

"He's only passed out, he'll be alright."

"You don't know that!" What if he was seriously injured? This was the first shapeshifter she'd been able to find, she couldn't let him die in the back of the truck the way Daniel had.

"Listen." Her dad sounded surprisingly sober now. "You want answers, right? You take him to the hospital, then there are doctors involved. Probably cops, too. They're gonna want all kinds of different answers, and you won't get yours. Take him to the motel room."

It sounded like a bad idea, but it had a certain logic, and Billie was too shaken to argue.

"Okay," Billie breathed. "Which is where?"

He pointed the direction to the motel, and Billie concentrated on trying to keep the wave of excitement and panic at bay while she drove. After a few minutes, she backed into the parking space in front of their room. The man—the shifter, Billie thought with a little surge of hope—was still under the tarp, and, fortunately, still breathing.

They got him inside and onto one of the beds without much trouble.

Billie tossed one of the bathroom towels over, and her dad wrapped it around the man's waist. The attempt at modesty was a moot point at this stage, but Billie thought it might put him more at ease when he woke up.

Now that he was, hopefully, safe in their room, Billie took a moment to actually look at him. Billie guessed he was late twenties. He had long dark hair down to his shoulders, and sharp, pointed features. Stubble covered his jawline and upper lip, as though he regularly shaved but hadn't had the chance in several days. Blood caked on a long cut across his forearm.

The coyote paw tattoo on his chest swelled and shrank with his sleeping breath. Did all of the shifters have something like that? Was it part of the initiation that Billie had missed by not growing up with a shifter family? Or had someone else had done that to him, to mark him, brand him? She rubbed a hand over her collarbone, drifting down to the skin above her right breast, imagining a cat print where this man had a dog print. Her mother hadn't had a paw print tattoo.

She was just about to ask her dad if he knew anything about the tattoo when he shoved a couple of twenty-dollar bills at her and told her to go to the 24-hour Wal-Mart they'd passed on the way and get some clothes and food. Billie protested at first, but one of them needed to do it. The man was tall enough that Billie's dad's clothes wouldn't fit him, and lean enough that Caleb's would have been way too big. Not that she had any of Caleb's clothes with her anyway. Besides, her dad was still drunk. He'd sobered enough to get this far, but he kept burping, and his words had become slurred and slow again.

She took one more look over her shoulder, eyes lingering on the coyote paw tattoo, before she pulled the motel door shut behind her. Maybe by the time she came back, he'd be awake and she could finally get some answers.

TUESDAY

At the store, Billie loaded a handcart with a pair of men's jeans, a pack of white t-shirts, and some cheap tennis shoes, guessing at the size. What was left of the money she used to buy as much junk food as she could—chips and beef jerky and a bag of off-brand cereal. A surly employee helped her struggle through using the self-checkout and it was after midnight by the time she got back to the motel room.

The stranger was still asleep in one bed, and her dad had passed out in the other one. Billie set the bags down on the table as quietly as she could, and looked between them. Her dad was on top of the covers, still fully dressed, with only his shoes kicked off. The man was under the covers now, the cut on his arm cleaned. He must have woken up while she was gone and decided he was safe enough here to go back to sleep. Billie snagged a pillow from her dad's bed, took it with her into the bathroom and, eventually, fell asleep in the bathtub.

She woke up to a spray of water. Her limbs flailed as she instinctively scrambled for escape like the cat she was, her heartbeat pounding and her brain taking a moment to catch up to what was going on. Someone else yelped. Billie came to her senses enough to realize she was still in the bathtub; someone else must have turned on the water, planning to take a shower. She groped for the faucet and shut the water off. Soaked, she climbed out and grabbed one of the towels from the rack above the toilet.

Through the bathroom door, she saw the man they'd rescued, bath towel around his waist. He whirled toward her, grabbing the empty coffee carafe from the table and brandishing it like a weapon.

"Who the fuck are you?"

Billie sighed and stepped out of the bathroom. She was only partially dry, but she slung the towel she'd been using over her shoulder and put her hands up. "It's okay," she stammered. "My dad… your dad…"

He stepped forward, practically growling now, "What have you done with my dad?"

Billie took a sudden step backward, bumping into the doorframe. "What? No, nothing! It's… he was missing, you were all missing, we were looking for all of you and we found you… you were passed out by the river, and… listen, I'm like you, okay?"

His expression softened as she spoke, but then he went back on edge just as quickly. He still wielded the carafe like he was ready to hit her over the head with it.

"What do you mean, *like me*?"

"I'm a…" God, why was it so hard to say? She'd kept the secret so long, from so many people. And she'd seen him in coyote form. She'd watched his shift happen before her eyes. He *was* like her. "I'm a shapeshifter. Like you. Like your family."

His eyes bored into her. He straightened to his full height, forcing Billie to look up at him. He was only a little taller than Caleb, and a whole lot leaner, but his intensity made him a formidable presence in that moment.

"Prove it," he barked after a tense minute.

"What?" Billie said.

"I say bullshit. Prove it."

Billie bristled. "I don't have to prove anything to you. I don't even know you."

"You want me to put down this... this..." He looked up at the carafe as though realizing how ridiculous a weapon it was, then lowered it by his side. "You want me to trust you're not one of them, I need to see it."

One of them? Who did he mean by *them?*

Billie paused a moment longer, then yanked off her shirt, shimmied out of her pajama pants, and threw them angrily on the floor. His eyes grazed appreciatively across her body, one side of his mouth quirked up, but she folded as quickly as she could, landing on cat's paws, a hiss already in her throat. He dropped the carafe, his towel falling, and he shifted too, suddenly a growling coyote. Billie breathed in his scent, memorizing it, gleaning as much information as she could about him. It was definitely the same not-quite-human, not-quite-animal scent she'd detected last night. Though he seemed to have recovered significantly with the night's rest, and the Scarlet undertone was far less pronounced. Still, if he had taken the drug, it meant he was dangerous. Potentially *very* dangerous.

The door swung open and Billie's dad came in, arms full of coffee cups and packaged muffins from the motel's continental breakfast.

"Whoa." He kicked the door shut behind him, but stayed pressed against it. Canine and feline circled each other. "Uh, guys?" he said after a moment. "I didn't pay the pet fee for this room, you know."

Billie flattened herself to the floor, ears back, still ready to pounce if she needed to. The coyote took a couple of steps back, stopped growling, and grinned at her, tongue lolling over sharp canines just like any other dog. He shifted back to human. Billie followed, gathering her clothes from the floor as quickly as she could. They were still wet, but she didn't want to take the time to get fresh clothes out of her bag.

Her dad set the coffee and muffins on the table, attempting to avert his eyes from both of them.

"Last night," the man said to Billie's dad, "you said you were a friend of my dad's."

"I am. Spent some time at your house last year. Think you were playing video games most of the time I was there."

"Dad doesn't... didn't... let many strangers in."

"And for good reason. I'm Keith Blackwater. And that's my daughter, Billie." He motioned toward Billie, who had gotten her shirt on, but was still struggling with the damp, twisted-up pajama pants.

Definitely one of the more awkward moments of my life, Billie thought. And yet, she felt exhilarated. His body had folded and unfolded from human to animal and back, just like her. There *were* other people like her in the world, and she'd finally found them.

Travis glanced over at Billie and suddenly seemed to realize he was just standing there with his cock out. He grabbed the towel from the floor to wrap it around himself. Billie's dad offered him the bag of clothes she'd bought.

"I remember you," he said to Billie's dad as he yanked tags off the clothes. "I'm Travis."

"Well, Travis," Billie's dad said, "I don't know what the hell is going on. But I can assure you, we're on your side."

Dressed now, Travis snagged a muffin and sat on the bed, unwrapping it. The jeans fit perfectly, but the t-shirt was a little tight, which, Billie had to admit, wasn't exactly a bad thing. He didn't have broad muscles like Caleb did, but he was toned and lean in a way Billie could appreciate. She could still see the dark outline of the coyote paw tattoo through the white fabric. After a moment, he crumpled the wrapper and looked straight at her. She darted her gaze away, a flush rising in her cheeks.

"I've never met anyone except our family who can shift," he said.

Billie was still sitting on the floor. She drew her knees into her chest and wrapped her arms around them.

"Me neither," she said. "I mean, I've never met *anyone* else. Except my mom."

Travis's gaze flicked quickly over toward Billie's dad. He knew the story, then. Billie pulled her knees in a little tighter.

"Does that mean you're related to us, then?" Travis asked, gaze darting back and forth between the two of them.

"I don't know," Billie answered. "That's part of what I wanted to find out."

Travis studied her face, an expression on his that she couldn't read. She felt her cheeks redden deeper and she reached up to pull on her hair, stringing it down over her face as if she could hide behind it.

"Her name was Valerie," she said. She looked to her dad, realizing she didn't even know what last name she'd had before she'd taken on Blackwater. He didn't volunteer a surname.

Travis shrugged. "Could be a cousin or something, I guess. Most of us stay pretty close, though. My dad would know." His expression darkened. "My dad. He's still in there. All of them are."

"In where?" Billie and her dad asked at the same time.

Travis grabbed another muffin and noisily unwrapped it, looking like he was trying to figure out how much to trust them with.

"We went to your house," Billie volunteered. "Everyone was gone, it looked like there was a struggle. What happened?"

After a long moment, Travis said, "Jeff went missing first." He nodded toward Billie's dad, narrowing his eyes again as though he wasn't fully cleared of suspicion. "Shortly after you left, actually."

Billie glanced at her dad. "Another of the kids," he clarified. "I mean, not *kid* kids, but, your brother?" he asked Travis.

Travis nodded. "Older brother. He was gone for a while—a couple of months, I guess. We were trying not to involve the cops, but we kind of ran out of options. So Dad went in to file the missing person's report. Someone was supposed to come out to the house to question all of us. But…"

He stared off into space for a long moment, until Billie softly said his name. "Um," he said, and scrubbed a hand over his face. "Some guys came. But it wasn't the cops. At least… anyway, they had some kind of chemical that they sprayed us with. We couldn't shift.

Couldn't protect ourselves."

Billie sucked in a breath. "There's a chemical that can stop us from shifting?"

Travis nodded grimly.

Which meant that the attackers had known what the Lesniks were. Billie hadn't been able to shift at their house—had the chemical still been in the air?

"Even in human form," Travis said, "some of us put up a decent fight. But they tranqued us. And when I woke up, I was… I don't know where I was. Someone's unfinished basement, I guess. They had me strapped to a chair with blood draining down a tube from my arm."

He touched his arm, and Billie could see marks from an IV on his inner elbow.

"So, what," Billie's dad asked, "vampires with a particular taste for shapeshifter blood?"

"Are vampires real?" Billie asked absently. She uncurled and stood up now, pacing the motel room.

"Hell, I don't know," her dad said. "I'm just trying to make sense of this whole thing." Then to Travis: "Was it vampires?"

"I don't… think so? Someone kept coming in to take the blood away and give me food. They kept spraying that chemical, but it finally wore off, and I was able to dig my way out."

"Was it Scarlet?" Billie asked. If Scarlet caused non-shifters to transform, maybe it had the opposite effect on shifters. She'd never taken the drug herself, but maybe simply being around it was what had caused her to lose her animal form that time in the forest, what kept her from shifting at the Lesnik's house. That could also explain why the scent was mixed with Travis's.

"What?"

"The chemical. Was it Scarlet that they sprayed you with?"

Travis looked between her and her dad, genuine confusion on his face. "I don't know what that is. So, maybe?"

She shook her head, filing away that hypothesis for now, and refocusing on what Travis could tell her.

"We found you by the river. How far did you run to get there?" Billie asked.

Travis took a long drink of coffee before he answered. "Last night's kind of a blur. But not far. A few blocks, maybe."

"Was it downtown?" It was the only part of town Billie knew anything about, but also, a detail from the ghost tour seemed suddenly relevant.

He thought for a second and then said, "Yeah, I guess it was."

"The coal storage," Billie said.

"Huh?" her dad asked.

"The ghost tour guy talked about these underground rooms below downtown Durango that used to be used for coal storage." She looked Travis. "Was that where they were keeping all of you?"

He shrugged. "It was underground, yeah. But I was there alone. I don't know what they did with everyone else."

"They could be in the other ones," Billie said.

"You think whoever did this would keep their hostages right there in the downtown?" her dad said skeptically.

Billie gestured at Travis. "He just said he hadn't run far—it was only a few blocks from downtown where we found him."

"And you don't have any idea who it was or why?"

"I have some suspicions about who," Travis said. "But I'm still pretty confused about the why."

"Who?" Billie's dad asked.

Travis swallowed the last of his second muffin. "The cop that my dad talked to. I heard his voice. And I could..." He glanced at Billie's dad unsurely. "I could smell him."

Billie nodded. Her senses were dulled in human form, but she still had a better nose than most people, and could distinguish some people's scents when they were distinctive enough.

"That means we can't go to the police about this," Billie said.

"Good," her dad said. Then to Travis, "Are you sure the others are still alive?"

He shook his head. "I'm not sure of anything. But I can't… I have to believe they're still alive."

"Is there anyone in town you trust, anyone who could help?"

Travis looked bewildered. "I'm not sure. I mean, we kind of kept to our own. We all have friends, but almost no one that knows what we are."

"Your sister!" Billie nearly shouted. *Of course.* "We should call Kaitlyn. She wasn't captured. We saw her yesterday. She's probably worried sick about all of you."

Travis frowned. "Kaitlyn. She's… we haven't been on the best terms."

"She's not a shifter," Billie said. "The only one of you who never learned."

Travis smirked. "It's not learned. You can do it, or you can't."

Billie's face flushed. She'd said it that way primarily to be polite, to make Kaitlyn's lack sound less like a disability. From her own experience, she knew that she could learn different forms, but the ability itself was instinctual, something that happened as naturally as breathing, something she longed and ached for if she spent too long in human form. "But she can't," she reiterated.

"She can't," Travis confirmed.

"We talked to her yesterday. She didn't seem to know you were all missing. I'm sure—whatever your relationship—she'll want to know you're safe. Unless you've got a better person to call?"

Travis shook his head.

Billie's dad picked up her phone from the bedside table and dialed Kaitlyn's number. "Voicemail," he said. Then, into the phone, "Hi, Ms., uh, sorry, *Professor* Lesnik. It's Keith Blackwater. I stopped by your office earlier. Got an update regarding someone in your family. Give me a call when you get the chance. Please."

He flipped the phone shut. Travis was working on the cereal now, eating whole handfuls.

"What do you want to do?" Billie asked. She knew what *she* wanted to do: charge downtown and yank open the door of every hidden underground room and free everyone trapped there. She also knew that was impossible and dangerous. It's not like she knew exactly where any of them were, and if they were below downtown shops, then there was no telling how many locals were involved with whatever was going on here. Just because she wanted to tear the place apart didn't mean it would do any good.

Travis swallowed a handful of cereal. "I want to go home," he said.

"Is it safe there?"

"I don't know. Probably not. But I need to at least get some of my own clothes and some important family things, if they're still there. Then find somewhere safe to hide out, while I figure out a way to free the others. If they're still alive."

"We'll get them out," Billie declared.

"I don't want you anywhere near that place!" her dad told her firmly.

Billie stopped pacing and turned to glare at him.

"We can't just leave them there!" she nearly shouted.

"This isn't your fight," her dad said.

She threw her arms up. "The hell it isn't! These people might be my family, too. Do *you* know where Mom came from? Since you didn't even bother to *ask* them if they knew her?"

After a tense moment, he said softly, "No, I don't. But there's someone out there kidnapping shapeshifters. I want to keep you safe, baby doll. I want to get you as far away from this as I can."

"And abandon these people you said were your friends?"

A flash of anger crossed his face, but faded just as quickly. To Travis, he said, "We'll take you out to your house."

At least it was a step in the right direction. Billie grabbed her bag and took it into the bathroom to change out of the damp pajamas.

Once she was changed, the three of them climbed into the truck. Billie was stuck in the middle, straddling the console and sitting rigidly to try to keep her legs from knocking against either her dad's or Travis's.

Travis leaned against the window, elbow propped up, head in his hands.

"Your tattoo," Billie said. Travis lifted his head and looked over at her. "Is that… like, a thing all of you have?"

He gave her a sad smile. "Most, yeah. Dad does it when we turn eighteen. He says the modern world makes it harder to shift, harder to be who we're meant to be. But even if we keep human form forever, the tattoo can be a reminder of who we really are, what we can do."

Billie absently touched the skin below her left collarbone.

"You're a bobcat," Travis said, and Billie squirmed a bit at the memory of their awkward interaction. "That's… different."

"Mom was a mountain lion," she said, and noticed her dad's hands grip harder on the steering wheel. "I managed it once, not long ago, but it's not how I'm comfortable."

"You can still do multiple forms?" Travis asked.

"Yeah," Billie said with surprise. "Not always well, but… You can't?"

Travis shook his head. "I mean, you play around, experiment as a kid. But then normally you settle into the one that fits best, and it just become second nature."

"Oh." Billie looked down at her hands. There was so much she didn't know. Had she been shifting wrong?

"That's pretty cool, that you can switch forms," Travis said.

She peeked shyly at him. "Yeah?"

He grinned at her, and it was the first time she'd seen him smile. It looked good on him, softened the sharpness of his features. "Yeah. What other shapes can you do?"

"Um, a dog," she said.

He raised an eyebrow, and his smile grew a little larger. "Really? What kind of dog?"

An ugly one, she almost said, remembering the awkward mangy thing she'd become to try to track the killer back in Juniper. But before she could answer, her dad pulled into the Lesniks' driveway and passed the open gate. Travis's face darkened again. He sat up straight, eyes taking in the mess of the front yard, the aftermath of his own kidnapping. The chickens were gone now, Billie noted. But everything else looked the same. Once her dad parked, Travis walked straight to the front door, and it opened easily, still unlocked. Billie hesitantly followed, and her dad lingered on the porch, keeping watch.

Travis went upstairs, and Billie wandered around the living room, examining all the photographs that lined the wall and mantle. She stared at a wedding photo, the faded and grainy colors indicating it was likely from the early 80s. Rather than a long wedding gown, the woman's dress was short and sleeveless, falling to mid-thigh, just above the tops of white go-go boots. A veil was thrown back over her hair, secured by a flowered headband, and the photographer had caught her laughing, her mouth open, eyes crinkled in joy. The man beside her was significantly taller, broad-shouldered and muscular. He had long hair and atrocious 70s-style sideburns. The top buttons of his white button-up shirt were open, showing off his chest hair. The background wasn't a church or a courthouse; it was the forest.

Most of the other photographs were newer, some of them including both of the parents and all five kids, some of them another group that was probably extended family. She searched for any faces that resembled her mother's. No such luck. Travis's mother's side of the family were dark-haired and olive-skinned, with high broad cheekbones and long, narrow noses, possibly Greek or Italian ancestry. Travis's dad's side were all tall and burly, still dark-haired, but paler-skinned. None of them looked anything like Billie's mother had: petite but broad-hipped, with light brown hair verging on auburn.

Billie sensed movement behind her and turned to see her dad leaning against the threshold between the living room and the kitchen.

"She's not here anywhere." She gestured to the photographs. Her dad shook his head.

"No, baby doll," he said sadly. "She isn't."

She glanced over at him. He'd said he hadn't asked the Lesniks if they'd known his wife, but Billie realized he'd probably looked at these photographs the exact same way she had.

"What was Mom's last name?" Billie asked. "Maiden name, I mean."

"Smith," he said.

Billie frowned. That certainly didn't narrow anything down.

Travis came back downstairs, carrying a silver lockbox. He still wore the jeans she'd bought, but he'd changed to a black t-shirt with a looser fit and some well-worn skater shoes. His hair was slightly damp and slicked back into a low ponytail.

She gestured vaguely toward the photographs. "I don't think I'm related to you."

"I sure hope not." Their eyes met and he gave a slight smile.

Billie was confused for a moment. *Oh shit*, she realized. *He's flirting with me!* And right in front of her dad, which was… awkward. And she had a boyfriend, which was… also awkward.

She turned back to the photographs, not quite in time to hide the flush on her cheeks. "How did your parents meet?" she asked. "Seems like it would be rare for two unrelated shapeshifters to find each other."

Then again, here she was with Travis. He sat on the couch and worked at the combination lock on the box. She stayed standing, over by the mantle, peeking over her shoulder at him. He'd taken after his mother's side, smooth olive skin, high cheekbones, and lean frame. His sleek black hair had a slight wave to it. In every way Caleb was blunt and broad, Travis was cut and trim.

Caleb.

Billie felt guilty for the warm flutter she felt in her stomach. Then a flash of anger, both at Caleb, and at herself for feeling guilty. They'd left on such uncertain terms that she didn't even know where she and Caleb stood at the moment. Caleb had slept with several other girls while he was in college. He'd told her, and she'd forgiven him, gotten over it, because that was in the past and he said he regretted it. He'd chosen her, and things were good between them. Or, they had been, until recently. But Billie had never been with anyone else. Juniper had a real shortage of attractive men around her age, not to mention the fact that it was so hard for her to trust anyone. But she should be able to simply enjoy looking at the man in front of her without feeling like she was doing something wrong.

Crap, he was talking, and here she was just... *admiring* him without actually listening. She turned all the way toward him and focused.

"It's a good story," Travis was saying. "But I want them to tell it to you."

He finally got the box open and pulled a piece of paper out, quietly shutting the lid.

"Me too," Billie said.

He picked up a smartphone and dialed a number. After a moment, he tossed the paper down and muttered, "Shit."

"What?" Billie asked.

Travis tapped the phone and tossed it onto the coffee table. "Dad always said if anything bad ever happened, we were supposed to call this number. But it was disconnected." He opened the box again, tossed the paper back inside. He grabbed a wad of bills from the box and stuffed them into a wallet.

"Now what?" Billie asked.

Travis leaned back on the couch, shaking his head.

"Lisa might know something about the tunnels," Billie's dad said.

She startled at his voice; she'd almost forgotten he was there.

"Tunnels?" Billie said.

"The underground rooms, whatever."

Thought you didn't want me anywhere near all that, Billie thought bitterly. But if he was willing to investigate more, she wasn't going to protest. She looked to Travis.

"Lisa Sieben?" he asked and her dad nodded. Travis locked the box and then carried it upstairs.

Billie turned her back on her dad, afraid he'd change his mind if she said anything at all. She studied what looked like the most recent family portrait. Kaitlyn wasn't in this one—she was only in a few of the photos, Billie noted. Travis stood in between two brothers, one older with short hair and a beard, the other a lanky teenager. His hands rested on the shoulders of a little girl with a big smile, showing a missing tooth. Quite the range in age from oldest to youngest.

"Let's go," Travis said when he came back down. This time, he locked the front door behind him.

Just as the three of them reached the truck, a deer stepped out from behind a tall stump. It was a fawn, with overlong legs and spotted back.

"Oh, my god, Samantha?" Travis shut the truck door and moved toward the deer. The deer's eyes flicked toward Billie and it took a step backward, ready to flee back into the forest at any second. Travis put a hand out and slowly approached the deer. "You can trust her. She's one of us."

The deer slowly, clumsily unfolded into a ten-year-old girl, dirt-smeared, with long ratty hair. The same girl, Billie was sure, from many of those photos she'd studied on the mantle. She had the lanky legs and arms of someone in the middle of a growth spurt, whose torso hadn't quite caught up to the rest. Billie's heart nearly skipped a beat. This girl was even younger than Billie had been when she'd lost her mother, but she carried the same kind of pain in her eyes. Travis placed his hands gently on her dark hair and kissed the top of her head. "You got away. I'm so glad you got away."

The girl looked up at her brother and suddenly burst into tears.

As soon as Caleb arrived at the quarry, he knew something was different. He could sense the stones around him, the way you might feel the presence of another person in the room before seeing them. There was a hum in the air, layers of vibrations. Each time a stone cracked under the pressure of the bulldozers and crushers, the vibration changed. Not necessarily a negative change—Caleb sensed no pain or loss. It just took on a different tone, split into variations of the original.

He tried to ignore it, shake it off. He figured the strange sensations would fade as the day wore on, but they only grew stronger. By the time he got back in the car to head home, he felt frazzled. The intensity lessened once he left the quarry, but a constant hum continued to underlie everything, as though the mountains themselves were buzzing. He didn't even go back to the cabin. Instead, he went straight to Chloe's.

She opened the door with a smile, but before she could even say hello, Caleb said, "What did you do to me?"

Her smile softened, not quite turning to a frown. "What?"

"The rocks," he said. "Stones. Everywhere. I... I feel them now."

Chloe shut the door quietly behind her and reached for his arm. But when she touched him, it wasn't the soft skin of her hand that he felt, but the pink polished stones of her bracelet that suddenly sang at him with an airy, high-pitched vibration. He flinched away.

"I told you I thought you had some magic in you." She was grinning again, elated. "I guess my healing yesterday sort of woke it up!"

"Okay, then," Caleb said, "put it... back to sleep. I guess. This is weird."

She laughed brightly. "There's no putting it back. And it only feels weird because it's new. I remember when mine first awakened. It's kind of like when you've never heard a word before, and then after you learn what it means, you start to see it everywhere. You'll get used to it."

"I don't want to get used to it."

She put both hands on his arms, and he didn't flinch away this time. The high-pitched vibration was somewhat less of a shock.

"It's earth magic, Caleb. It's a connection that our ancestors used to have. That we're *supposed* to have. It might be louder now, but you can't tell me you've never felt hints of it before."

"I…" Caleb faltered. It was true that he had always had an affinity for stones. As a kid, he'd constantly been picking up rocks. He'd been grounded for it once by his mom, before she got ill, because she said all the pebbles left in his pockets were going to destroy her washing machine. As a teenager, he'd worn choker necklaces with lapis lazuli beads and onyx pendants. He'd majored in geology in college, instead of business like his dad had wanted him to.

"Some, sure," he admitted. "But… not like this."

Chloe nodded. "I have a little consultation at Enchanted Mountain today. Come with me. Maybe Heather can teach you how to control it."

"Is that how you learned?"

"I have an aunt who taught me a little. But mostly just lots of books. I can give you some of those too." She gave his arms a friendly squeeze. "Let's go talk to Heather. Billie told me she was the real deal. Can you drive me?"

"Uh?"

"Say yes. Come in for a moment, let me grab my purse."

Caleb hesitated, but she held the screen door open for him and he caved and followed her inside. Luke sat on the couch—they'd removed the plastic film, finally—yelling at a baseball game on TV.

Chloe gave Luke a kiss. "Caleb's going to take me to see my witch friend."

"Okay, sweetie." As she left the room, Luke rolled his eyes and made a "cuckoo" motion.

Caleb felt awkward as shit, but Luke gave no indication that he had a problem with another guy driving his wife into town.

"Ready?" Chloe emerged from the bedroom with a tiny vinyl purse. Luke was already yelling at the umpire again.

Just as they parked in front of the Enchanted Mountain Metaphysical Shop, Mouse came racing down the center of Miners Avenue, some ragged animal chasing after him.

"Is that...?" Chloe trailed off.

"A beaver, yeah," Caleb said.

Although, the way it snarled it almost looked more like a wolverine, and its fur was starting to slough off like the deer's had. A whole tray of Scarlet vials clinked in Mouse's arms. The drug-addled beaver stayed right on his heels. A couple of tourists filmed the spectacle from a bench in front of Robyn's real estate office.

If Mouse was running with the Scarlet, that meant he'd figured out that's what the creatures were after. But where the hell was he going with it? He made a sudden turn and darted between buildings. The beaver slipped on the asphalt, landed on its side, then recovered and dove after him. Caleb slammed the car door behind him, ignoring Chloe's shrieks of protest.

Mouse jumped down a small staircase, landing in a judo roll that somehow managed to keep the tray upright. But then he did the very thing Caleb had been afraid he might: he flung the tray into the river.

Several vials smashed against the rocks, bleeding their poison right into the water. Others submerged intact. The beaver leaped past and dove in after them. Apparently sated, it floated downstream.

Mouse raised his fists in triumph. Caleb jumped the last few stairs. He grabbed Mouse's arm and spun him around.

"You idiot!" Caleb yelled. "Do you have any idea what you just did?"

"Hey, get off me." Mouse tried to yank his arm free, but Caleb was far stronger. He pushed Mouse away with an exasperated growl and waded into the river.

Caleb braced to keep his balance; the river flowed fast and ice cold with fresh snowmelt from the higher peaks nearby. All the Scarlet vials had been washed out of sight, on their way right to the lake. Caleb waded back to shore.

Chloe rushed up to him. "Oh my god, I thought you might get hurt. That beaver was like the deer, wasn't it?"

Caleb nodded gravely. "So you said what we have is earth magic, right?"

She looked baffled, but nodded.

"Is there water magic? People who can purify water?"

She shrugged. "Might be. I don't know any."

Damn. "This is going to keep happening until the water gets, I don't know, cleaned up somehow." And now that Mouse had dumped a whole bunch more into the river, how much worse was it about to get?

The tourists who had been filming the incident had apparently lost interest, but a few of the locals had gathered on the riverbank, Joaquin among them.

"We'll get together a hunting group, like we did for the killer cat a couple of weeks ago," Joaquin was saying.

Caleb was surprised Joaquin hadn't already taken to just walking around with a rifle after the deer incident. He sat on the bottom step and yanked his boot off, pouring out river water.

"I told Randall about the deer," Joaquin said to Caleb, "but he didn't want nothing to do with it. I don't get it."

"He got in some legal trouble for the lion, didn't he?" someone else in the crowd suggested.

Caleb bit his tongue. There had been no killer cat, and he suspected the mountain lion that Joaquin's hunting party had taken down had been brought in and planted for that purpose, to deflect attention from the true killer. The news had revealed that the cat could be traced to exotic animal traders, after all.

"This town has been beset by demons," a voice declared from the top of the stairs. Caleb turned to see Reverend Provine slowly making his way down. Caleb shoved the wet boot back on his foot and got out of the way. "You cannot hunt these creatures with earthly weapons. There is only one way to truly banish this scourge."

"I shot one yesterday," Joaquin said. "*Earthly weapons* work just fine on them."

The reverend gave him a pitying look. "Do they, though? The demon didn't die, it only took a different form, possessed a different body. I suppose we could rain death down on this valley, and let the devil jump from corpse to corpse."

Joaquin opened his mouth, then closed it, scratched his head. He glanced back uncertainly toward the river. The beaver was long gone by now, but everyone looked around as though expecting more demon animals to leap out at any moment.

"Oh, this is ridiculous," Caleb said. "They're after the Scarlet. Right?" He turned to Mouse, but Mouse raised his hands and said, "Hey, I don't know what you're talking about." Caleb glared at him. *Should have nicknamed him Weasel instead.*

The reverend nodded soberly. "Indeed. Drugs are one of the devil's favorite tools. They make the mind vulnerable to invasion."

"That's not—" Caleb groaned. "Whatever." His shoes were soaked, and he needed to get away from this kind of idiocy. He stomped up the staircase.

"Mr. Mulligan." Caleb turned with a sigh. "Is there a reason you have been present at two of these incidents?"

"Funny you should use the word 'reason' while you're accusing me of being in league with the devil." He stabbed a finger in the direction of the river. "That shit that Mouse just dumped in the river is what causes the transformation. It's weird, but it's just some type of biological response to the drug."

The reverend gave him an appraising look, and then turned to the small gathered crowd and began preaching more about how only the power of prayer and repentance could save Juniper. Caleb climbed the rest of the way to the top of the staircase.

Chloe hurried after him. "Um," she said, a little shake in her voice. "I didn't think this was a real churchy type town."

Caleb leaned against the car and took off the other boot. There was even more water in this one. "It's not, generally. But when people get spooked, they start looking for answers, I guess." He motioned toward the shopfront of Enchanted Mountain. "You should go ahead. I need to go get changed. Come by the cabin when you need a ride back home after."

Chloe glanced uncertainly at the store, then back in the direction of the group. The reverend was still talking, but Caleb couldn't hear what he was saying from here.

"They're not going to come burn the place down to purge the town of witches, are they?" she asked.

"Hard to say, honestly." He knew Billie had suffered some harassment, accusations of being a witch from people who didn't understand what had happened to her mother, but it had never escalated to physical violence. Then again, people were always more likely to do terrible things as part of a group, especially when their already existing prejudices were heated by a fanatic flame.

"If they go full pitchfork mob," Chloe said, "I feel like Enchanted Mountain will be one of the first targets."

Caleb was starting to think he and Billie's cabin might be a likely target, because of all that history, but he could see Chloe's point as well. He shoved his wet boot back on. "Okay. I'll keep watch at the door while you have your consultation."

"Yay!" She gave a little hop of excitement and grabbed his hand. "Thank you."

He meant outside the shop, but Chloe kept hold of his hand and pulled him in after her. The door chime dinged, and the scent of patchouli assaulted his nostrils. So did the discordant vibrations of a dozen different gemstones. He balked. Chloe turned, confused, but then followed his gaze to the wooden buckets full of polished rocks and crystals.

"See, this is why you need to learn," she said.

"Later," he said, stepping all the way inside.

Heather moved a bead curtain aside as she emerged from the back room. She glanced at a pocket watch and snapped it shut, plunking it back into a shirt pocket.

"You must be Chloe Sieben."

"I am," Chloe said brightly. She let go of Caleb, rushed up to the counter, and extended her hand. "It is *so* nice to meet you."

Heather looked past Chloe to Caleb, who lingered closer to the door. "Caleb Mulligan," she said, a note of surprise in her voice. "Can I help you find something?"

"Oh, he just gave me a ride," Chloe answered for him.

Heather raised an eyebrow and glanced between them. "I see. Billie's still out of town?"

"Um." Caleb shifted in his wet boots. "Yes, ma'am."

It's not like that, Caleb wanted to tell her, but honestly, he didn't quite know what it was like or not. Chloe was beautiful and interesting. She was bright and bubbly in all the ways Billie was dark and melancholy. He was still mad at Billie for leaving, but that didn't mean he was going to leave her or cheat on her. Even if Chloe was a temptation. He picked up a book from the shelf and said, "I'm just going to browse while you ladies do your thing." *And try to keep the fanatics from breaking your windows,* he didn't say.

Heather seared him with one more judgmental glare, and then shifted her attention back to Chloe. "Well. Let's get started, shall we?" She lifted the bead curtain and gestured for Chloe to follow her into the back.

Caleb looked down at the book he'd grabbed. *Astral Travel to Other Planets.* He flipped through it for a second, past descriptions of complicated breathing techniques and drawings of souls floating away from bodies while attached by an umbilical-like cord. Did people really believe this crap? He snapped the book shut and slid it back onto the shelf. And yet, who knew? The stones kept singing to him. Not quite an audible sound, not quite a tactile feel, but somewhere just in between. He'd experienced Chloe's healing firsthand, and he'd seen Billie shapeshift with his very own eyes. Maybe it *was* real—all of it.

He wandered toward the display of stones. The quartz wands and crystal balls and sparkling chunks of Fool's Gold were nearly silent. But most of the others vibrated in a quiet chorus. A cluster of unpolished copper pulsed at him like a heartbeat. Some malachite chimed like a cash till. A polished onyx sang a soft lullaby that somehow reminded him of his mother's voice. He reached toward the onyx, a little afraid of what might happen when he touched it.

But nothing exploded, no shocks burst through him. Instead, the stones' songs quieted, and calm flushed through his body.

The relief was short-lived, however, as his relaxed slump sent a bunch of bottles and figurines on the shelf behind him toppling over.

"Shit," Caleb muttered. He slipped the onyx into his jeans' pocket. He hurried to pick up the bottles of essential oils and colloidal silver, and to right all the Shiva and Ganesha statues he'd accidentally knocked over. The metals in the statues each had unique vibrations as well, he noticed, but all of the sensations were duller now, not quite so overwhelming and distracting as they had been before he touched the onyx. He picked up a small sign that had fallen down, which listed the many supposed healing properties of colloidal silver, but he couldn't figure out where the sign had fallen from, so he stuck it in between the bottles.

A few minutes later, the bead curtains rustled and Chloe and Heather emerged. Heather was asking her about scheduling another session, but to Caleb's surprise, Chloe was being evasive.

"Ready?" she asked him.

"Yeah. Oh." He pulled the onyx out of his pocket and set it on the counter, then dug his wallet out.

"Ah, black onyx," Heather said. "Helps to dispel negative energies, you know."

"I…" Caleb paused and cleared his throat. "I just think it's pretty."

"I bet you do." Heather gave another raise of her eyebrow as she handed him his change. He scooped the black stone up and turned away from the counter.

"Thanks again!" Chloe chirped on their way out the store.

Once they were back in the car, Caleb asked, "What happened? No luck?"

Chloe chewed her lip. "She's got… *something* going on. But it's different from us, and honestly I don't think it's very honed."

Caleb nodded like he understood what she meant, though he had no idea. He did a u-turn and started back toward Chloe's house.

"Helps, doesn't it?" she said.

"What?"

She gestured toward the onyx, which he'd been rolling around in the fingers of his left hand like a worry stone. He closed his palm over it.

"Onyx," she said. "That's interesting. Tells me a few things about you."

"Yeah? Like what?"

"You've got grief lingering around you. Something dark in your past, troubles regarding your family. Short temper, probably. Strong-willed, but reluctant to make big decisions by yourself."

Well, he couldn't exactly argue with any of that, much as he might want to.

"So," he said. "You have, like, a favorite?"

"Rose quartz." She held up her arm, indicating the small pink stones on her bracelet.

"And what should that tell me about you?"

She shrugged. "I have a book to give you. Read it and you might figure a few things out."

They were back at her house by now. Caleb put the car into park and Chloe removed her seatbelt.

"You want to come in? Hang out for a while?"

"Nah. I can feel the blisters getting bigger every second I spend in these wet boots."

"Oh. Right. Hold on, I'll be back." She stepped out and returned a few moments later, leaning into the open window to hand him a book. Caleb took the book, but then put more effort into figuring out where to stash it than was strictly necessary, to avoid being drawn in by the very appealing cleavage on display from the way she leaned in the window. "Thanks for not letting the townsfolk burn me at the stake," she said. It was a joke, but also, he got the sense, kind of not.

"Anytime."

She stepped away and he reversed down the narrow curving driveway.

Once home, he scrolled through the unanswered texts he'd sent to Billie. It wasn't unusual for her to not respond right away, but it had been almost a whole day. Before that, she'd sent some message that was barely decipherable. It wasn't unreasonable to expect a brief check-in, at least. That was what normal couples would do, wasn't it? Though, maybe she'd decided they weren't a couple anymore. Maybe she'd taken him at his word that he might not be here when she got back. Honestly, he wasn't sure how he felt about that.

He dialed her number, and his irritation grew with every ring. When it went to voicemail, he took a breath, then snapped his mouth shut and ended the call. He set the phone aside. God, he could even sense the gold and copper and lithium inside the phone. It was so strange. He reached for the onyx again, and then for the book Chloe had given him, flipping it open to the page about rose quartz.

Travis took Samantha into the house and sent her to take a shower and get dressed. While she did that, they discussed the best plan, deciding that, for now, Travis and Samantha would get a room in the same motel as Billie and her dad. But when Samantha came downstairs, dressed in flannel pajamas and her wet hair sloppily braided, Travis told her to pack an overnight bag, and she started crying again. It turned into a tantrum—complete with screaming, throwing things, and locking herself in her room. Billie and her dad waited awkwardly in the living room while Travis tried to negotiate with the girl.

Eventually, Travis came back downstairs. His hair was a mess, as though he'd been clutching at it in frustration.

"She's pretty traumatized," he said. "But she's also just being a brat. In any case, I think staying home with her will be best. You're both welcome to stay too, if you like."

Billie glanced at her dad, who looked lost in thought. "I really don't think we should leave you here alone," she said, and waited for her dad to agree.

"Yeah," he said, snapping out of it after a minute. "We'll stay." He stood up and grabbed the truck keys off of the coffee table. "Let me go check out of the motel and get our stuff. If Lisa's still around, I'll find out what she knows about the underground rooms. You okay here for an hour or so, you think?"

"Pretty sure," Travis said. And although Billie wasn't, that seemed to be enough reassurance for her dad to take off, leaving them there alone.

Samantha emerged from upstairs. "I'm going to watch cartoons," she declared, chin high as though daring either Travis or Billie to defy her.

Travis tossed the remote to her, and she caught it easily. "Go for it, kid. No screen time limits for now." Then to Billie, he said, "Would you mind helping me clean the place up?"

"Sure," she said. It would give her something to do other than feel so restless, at least, keep her from running through all the worst scenarios in her head over and over.

So Travis and Billie worked together to clean the house up—tossing the rotten kitchen trash, scraping food off the abandoned dishes, righting knocked-over chairs, opening the windows to air out the stale smells.

"Shouldn't your dad be back by now?" Travis asked as the sun began to dim behind the trees. Samantha had fallen asleep watching TV and Travis had carried her upstairs. Now he sat on the couch next to Billie, the TV still on but the volume down.

"He's probably still with *Lisa*," Billie said bitterly.

"What do you have against her?" Travis asked. "I mean, don't get me wrong, she's a weird lady, but she's pretty harmless."

She's not my mom, Billie thought. And then, after she struggled to find an excuse or snarky response, she went ahead and just said it: "She's not my mom."

"Ah," Travis said. "Do you want to call him?"

"No phone. Do you know Lisa's number?"

He shook his head. "We could call the place she works, though."

Billie held up her little flip phone with a shrug. "No internet on this thing to look it up."

He found the hotel number on his smartphone and read it off to her. When the clerk answered, Billie asked if they could put Lisa on.

"Is my dad there?" she asked once Lisa picked up the phone.

"He is, hon, but he's had a bit of liquid courage, if you know what I mean. Don't worry, I'll make sure he gets home safe."

Billie mumbled a thanks and hung up the phone. "Just as I thought. He's dead drunk. I don't think he's coming back tonight." *Typical.* Now she was stuck here.

"You're welcome to pick a room," Travis said. "We've got plenty, upstairs."

"I'm exhausted, but I'm also restless," Billie said. She'd had enough trouble sleeping at the motel, and now in this stranger's house she couldn't imagine relaxing enough to actually fall asleep.

"Yeah, me too," Travis said. He stood and suddenly pulled his shirt off. He hooked a thumb toward the back door. "I'm going to go for a run. You want to come?"

"I… you mean?"

"Of course."

"Is it safe?"

He tossed the shirt onto the couch. "Nothing is ever safe anymore. That doesn't mean we can't have a few moments of peace."

"But, Samantha…"

He glanced at the ceiling. "We'll sniff around the perimeter first, and stick to a path where we can see if any vehicles pull up." He shrugged. "You don't have to come. Just thought you might want to."

Billie's heart pounded, and her hands shook as she pushed herself up to stand. Travis grinned. He slid his pants off and headed toward the back door, comfortable in his own skin in a way Billie never had been. She admired him as much for that as she did for his lean fitness. She stayed dressed until she was out on the back porch. Travis looked back at her in coyote form now, eyes shining in the moonlight. Billie left her clothes in a pile on the back porch, and then she folded her body and landed with soft dirt beneath her paws. The coyote yipped and turned, racing toward the trees. Billie ran after him.

They looped the perimeter a few times, noses to the ground, but found nothing to indicate unwanted visitors were lurking. After a couple of laps, Travis started up a barely discernable trail near the locked gate. She couldn't keep up, but Travis occasionally looped back around or stopped to let her catch up. A couple of times, she lost sight of him, but she could follow his scent trail instead. This forest was different than the one she knew in Juniper, but it was still the forest, still pine trees and aspen and lichen and granite. The air was thick with the scent of nightbirds and chipmunks and other wild creatures. A stream burbled down the slope they climbed.

At the top, Billie collapsed on her side, panting, happy—exhilarated—from the run. When she caught her breath, she sat up to see Travis, back in human form, seated on an outcropping, dark hair loose around his shoulders. Billie unfolded as well. Her nighttime vision was dulled in human form, and she blinked into the sudden darkness for a moment before she adjusted. The moon was nearly full, and after a moment, the world came back into focus: the silhouettes of the trees, the skin of Travis's back practically glowing.

She climbed up and sat next to Travis. "Oh, wow." The spot overlooked a valley. A narrow waterfall to their left stair-stepped down smooth stone, flowing into the stream they'd followed. Below, Billie could just make out the porch light and outline of the house, but beyond that was a vast stretch of wilderness. She pointed toward a pyramid-shaped mountain in the distance, outlined by the last light of dusk. "Someone was telling me that mountain was a landing place for UFOs."

Travis barked a laugh. "I think I'd have seen some UFOs by now if that were true."

"The world is stranger than we think." Billie tried to say it seriously, but the absurdity of the UFO theory overcame her and she burst out laughing.

Travis grinned at her and reached over to rub a hand across her back. She leaned into his touch. She was just about to ask him if he'd traveled to many other places, but then she realized. She'd *leaned into his touch*. A handshake or casual brush against even someone she knew could stress her out, but here this man she had known for hardly a day had placed his hand on her bare back, and she felt okay with it. Better than okay.

With Caleb, she not only tolerated his touch, but craved it, couldn't get enough of. This wasn't *quite* the same as Caleb, but it felt comfortable. Welcome. She let Travis's hand rest on her skin a moment longer, but now that she was overthinking it, she was getting more uncomfortable by the second, more aware of her own nudity, of his, of the chill night air on all this exposed human skin.

She rippled, folded, and her spotted fur wrapped around her comfortable animal shape. Travis kept his hand on her back as she shifted—which was also new and strange—and gave her a friendly little pat and scratch before he shifted back to coyote. They ran together for a while longer, exploring this forest that was familiar and yet unfamiliar all at the same time. Billie followed him the way she used to follow her mother, trusting him to know where they were going so she could lose herself in the wildness of the moment. Eventually, he led her back to the house.

They unfolded together on the back porch, and almost as soon as they were both human again, his lips were on hers. Billie opened her mouth with a little "oh" of surprise and his tongue lapped gently at hers. She softened as a chill of pleasure rippled through her, and brushed her hands lightly across his shoulder blades. Travis pulled away and rested his forehead against hers. His hair tickled her cheek.

"I…" she said breathlessly. "I… have a boyfriend."

He lifted his head and stepped back. Billie reluctantly let her hands slide away from him. "Oh." Even in the dark, the flicker of disappointment across his face was obvious.

At least, I think I do, Billie thought.

He turned and opened the door, disappearing inside the house. Billie bit her lip and crossed her arms over her chest. She fumbled her way back into her clothes and then followed him inside.

"Travis?" she whispered. She heard a creak of floorboards upstairs and the slam of a door.

Damn. She touched a hand lightly to her cheek, the pleasant memory of his skin and his lips still fresh, feeling sad and excited and confused all at once.

He'd said to pick a room upstairs, but that felt like someone else's territory, and she ran the risk of opening the wrong door and finding herself in his arms again. Better if she stayed on the couch. She opened her phone and saw she'd missed a call from Caleb about an hour before. Even if it hadn't been nearly midnight, she didn't think she could bring herself to talk to him right now.

WEDNESDAY

A buzzing noise drew Billie out of a beautiful dream about running in the moonlight. She groaned a protest at the assault of the real world on her perfect moment. Why couldn't it always be that simple? Why did humans have to muck everything up with emotions and rules and relationships?

She fumbled for the phone on the coffee table and looked at it bleary-eyed, not recognizing the number. Normally she let strange numbers go to voicemail, but something told her to answer. It could be her dad, needing some kind of help. Or someone telling her Caleb had been in an accident.

"Hello?" she mumbled.

"Hello," a clipped feminine voice replied. "Is Mr. Blackwater available?"

"Mister…" Billie repeated with confusion. "Uh, this is *Miss* Blackwater. Who is this?"

"Doctor Kaitlyn Lesnik. I'm returning a call from yesterday."

"Oh." Billie sat upright, head clearing. "Yeah, um, we have your brother. I mean, that came out a lot more sinister than I meant. Your brother is safe. Travis. He's at your… he's at the house."

There was a rather long pause, long enough that Billie pulled the phone away from her ear and looked at the screen to make sure it was still connected. Then Kaitlyn said, "Well, that is a relief. Is that all?"

"Yes." Billie remembered the little girl, Samantha, and wondered if she should mention that she was safe too, but for some reason she opted not to. Kaitlyn's formality made Billie uncomfortable, and she felt like every word she spoke made the other woman think less and less of her. "I just… we just thought you'd like to know."

"You thought correctly. Thank you for informing me."

"You're welcome," Billie mumbled and then hung up as quickly as she could. At least that was done. Kaitlyn might not have the warmest relationship with her sibling, but she had surely been a lot more worried than she let on.

The rest of the house was silent, Travis and Samantha still asleep upstairs. Billie went into the bathroom, the one where she'd tried to shift the first time she'd come into the house. A faint metallic smell hung in the air. She was surprised she hadn't noticed that the first time. But then, everything had been strange, every sight and smell out of place, her senses overwhelmed with the mystery of this abandoned house. Now, she'd adjusted to the normal scents of this house, this family, even though they were mostly absent. And this chemical smell definitely didn't fit the normal scent profile of the house. She wrinkled her nose and considered going in search of a different bathroom, but she didn't want to wake the others, didn't want to accidentally stumble into Travis's space. So she flipped the light switches until she found one that turned on a fan, and then started the shower.

She had no clean clothes—either her dad had her bag with him or it was still back at the motel—but it still felt good to rinse away the last few days. She stayed in there for longer than she needed to, letting the water drain over her hair, until the room was full of steam and condensation dripped down the walls. She felt better when she stepped out—clearer headed, refreshed. And even better, the metallic chemical smell had dissipated. Billie used the towel to wipe a clear spot in the mirror and shifted only her eyes. It came easily this time, her irises going yellow, pupils stretching, her senses suddenly sharpening. She grinned at her reflection. Her canines were long and sharp, looking almost vampiric in her human face. She released the light folds, let her features snap back to fully human, and took her time getting dressed and towel drying her hair.

Travis and Samantha were both in the kitchen when Billie opened the bathroom door. Samantha smiled up at her from a bowl of cereal. Travis spent way more time looking in the refrigerator than he probably needed to before he gave her a cursory glance and a mumbled, "Hey."

Billie poured herself some cereal and talked to Samantha, trying to ask her about normal, mundane things. The girl chatted about her favorite cartoons and why she liked this cereal more than the other one on the counter. And then she said something about how her brothers always teased her about the food she liked, and then she got very quiet, and Billie couldn't figure out how to draw her out again. After a while, Samantha put her bowl in the sink and went upstairs again, leaving Billie and Travis seated next to each other at the table.

"Listen," Billie said after an awkward moment. "About last night…"

"There's nothing to talk about," Travis said.

"I think there's a *lot* to talk about," Billie said.

"There's not. It was just a swing and a miss. That's okay. You've got your life. I just thought…"

He trailed off. Billie watched him for a moment, appreciating the sharp lines of his face, the depth of the golden brown of his eyes. The memory of his lips on hers surged forth, so vivid it was almost like it was happening again. Her hands itched to reach over and touch him. She resisted at first, but after a moment, she went for it. She slid her hand over his forearm. He looked up at her, but didn't pull away. Billie closed her eyes, partially from embarrassment, partially because connecting both their skin and their eyes might be too overwhelming.

Billie took a deep breath in, trying to figure out why this felt comforting like Caleb, yet different. Caleb's touch gave her a sense of relief, like he drew out all of her pain, her grief, her loneliness, all that darkness and heaviness that she always carried around with her. He took all that away for a few moments, leaving only her true, radiant self.

Travis's touch didn't take anything away. Instead, it was almost as though she could feel the heat of his energy flowing into her skin, filling her with a warm, welcome glow. Caleb was lightness: the relief of a heavy weight suddenly removed. Travis was more like a warm, weighted blanket. Opposite approaches for a similar result. She could only imagine what it might feel like to be completely covered by him…

"I just thought…" Travis was saying, and Billie pulled her hand away from his arm so she could concentrate, swallowing the little gasp that threatened to expose where her mind had been starting to wander. "I've never met a girl who was a shifter. Aside from my family. We always have to be so careful around other people. I always wanted to find someone I could just be totally free with."

"I understand," Billie said in a small voice. And she really did. Caleb knew what she was, but he still turned away in discomfort when she folded into animal form. He still asked her awkward questions that showed he feared her powers and didn't understand her true nature. She couldn't ever run with him through the forest like she'd done with Travis. As far as she knew, Caleb was about as mundane human as you could get.

"I wanted to meet you—all of you—" Billie said, "because I wanted to be around people who were like me. Last night… last night was amazing. All of it. I just need to figure some things out."

"Forget it." Travis stood abruptly, scraping the chair behind him.

"Travis, I…" He turned to her, but she didn't actually know what to say. A cruel hardness passed over his face when she couldn't finish the sentence, and he turned away and went back upstairs.

Billie did the dishes, mostly to have something to do, her mind a jumble, going over the conversation again and again, trying to figure out what she could have said. If she was sure about what was happening between her and Caleb, this would be so much easier. Wouldn't it?

She had finally decided on what she was going to say to Travis when a truck rumbled into the Lesniks' driveway, parking just out of view from the windows above the sink. *Must be my dad*, Billie thought. *Finally*. She wiped the dish soap from her hands on the plaid kitchen towels.

A car door slammed. Footsteps pounded from the second level of the house and then down the stairs.

"Billie, run!" Travis shouted. He was tugging Samantha behind him, and the girl was already starting to shift, her legs buckling into spindly deer legs.

"What?" Billie said. "It's just my dad."

But they were already gone. The back door swung on its hinges. Billie went toward the front door, intending to look out the window there and confirm that it was her dad before letting him in, but the deadbolt was already turning. Someone with a key was opening the door. Billie backpedaled after Travis and Samantha, but stopped and turned back when she recognized Kaitlyn Lesnik's voice.

It's just their sister, Billie thought with relief. But Kaitlyn was flanked by two men. And one of them was...

"Elliot?" Billie said incredulously. "Elliot Moran?" Toby Moran's cousin, who she'd seen at the funeral back in Juniper. What was he doing here?

There was something cruel in the grin that spread over Elliot's face. Billie walked backward, bumping into furniture, her skin already rippling.

"Get rid of her," Kaitlyn said.

"She's a shifter, too," Elliot said.

"Oh?" Kaitlyn said. "Well in that case..."

She raised a small pistol and shot.

Billie had no time to run. She flinched, but the sound was a small pop, not a true gunshot, and she looked down in disbelief at the small dart protruding from her chest. She plucked it out and tossed it away as if it were a spider, and started to shift as she ran toward the back door, letting her clothes stretch and tear. But before she could reach the back door, one of the men engulfed her in a chemical spray, and Billie stopped cold, the shift incomplete, part woman and part cat. She howled with the excruciating pain of it, and the sound was both caterwaul and scream, somewhere in between, both and neither. She tried to finish the shift, but it was like trying to fold a piece of paper too many times. Gradually, painfully, the folds released, and her human form returned in full. Her eyesight began to blur, a fog descending over all her senses as the tranquilizer from the dart took effect. She blinked up at Kaitlyn, Elliot, and the other man before darkness overwhelmed her.

The sharp chemical smell came first, the burn of it in her nose. Billie coughed, gasped for breath, tasted blood and bile and the chalkiness of dust and dirt. The burn of something wrapped around her wrist came next, the cold hardness of the chair beneath her, the chill of stone below her bare feet.

Billie groaned and opened her eyes. A kerosene lamp burned in a corner, dimly lighting the rough stone bricks, the rusty metal beams.

"Welcome back, Miss Blackwater." Kaitlyn Lesnik sat in a second chair across from Billie.

Billie tried to no avail to pull her arms free, and hissed at a sudden pinch in her inner elbow. They were pumping something into her. No, they were *taking* something. A crude IV drained her blood down a tube.

Kaitlyn stood and held something out, pushing it toward Billie's face. She turned her head away, tried to shift, wanting to snap at Kaitlyn with sharp teeth. But she was stuck, just a cardboard doll, and each attempted fold drained her energy more and more.

"I'm trying to help you, you ungrateful bitch," Kaitlyn said. "You don't want to starve down here, do you?"

Billie resisted a moment longer, but then stopped struggling, out of energy, and opened her mouth. It was a graham cracker, sweet and tart, and every bite was an effort to chew and swallow. Kaitlyn gave her some water from a plastic bottle next, and it was shockingly cold, sending a chill through Billie's teeth and up her skull like an ice cream headache.

"There," Kaitlyn said. "That's not so bad, is it?"

"You fucking kidnapped me," Billie rasped. "Of course it's bad."

Kaitlyn screwed the cap back on the bottle. "We could have killed you. Good thing my associate knew you'd be useful instead."

"How did he…" Billie started.

But then she knew how. Back in Juniper, at the cemetery. It had been Elliot's son who had called her a witch, and she'd scared him away by shifting only her eyes and teeth. *No one would believe a kid,* she'd rationalized. But if Elliot already knew that shifters were real, then he *would* believe what his kid said she'd done.

"Why?" she croaked out instead.

Kaitlyn said nothing, but almost as soon as Billie asked the question, the clues began to slot together.

"Scarlet," Billie guessed. She'd caught the faint scent of it near the underground rooms where the shifters were being kept. Where— Billie realized—*she* was now being kept. She'd smelled it on Travis, although he claimed not to know what it was. Kaitlyn was working with Elliot Moran, who had been Toby Moran's supplier—the one who had brought Scarlet into Juniper and set off the whole chain of events with Daniel Gadbury. And the final piece of the puzzle, which suddenly made everything fit: at the hospital, when Billie had tried to donate blood to Caleb, they'd told her she had Scarlet in her system even though she'd never taken the substance. "There's something in shifter blood that goes into making Scarlet."

"Quite clever deduction for someone who probably barely graduated eighth grade," Kaitlyn said.

"Do you know what that stuff does to people?"

Kaitlyn shrugged. "It's a work in progress. As long as idiots keep buying it, I can keep working on my research."

"Which is," Billie reasoned, "to be able to shift yourself."

"A-plus," Kaitlyn said facetiously. "But not solely for myself, of course. There are plenty of broad applications."

"But they're your family," Billie said. "You kidnapped your own family."

"My *family*—" A surge of anger spread over Kaitlyn's face. "—thought I was a disgrace, a mistake. I told people about them when I was a child. I told everyone what they were. But no one believed me. I was just that weird, crazy little girl. Then my teacher finally did believe me—she said it was possible, but had never been proven. I took her to my house, but they wouldn't show her. They told her I made things up for attention, turned her against me just like everyone else. So don't act like you know anything about my family." Kaitlyn stared into space for a moment, then shook her head like she was clearing away bad memories. She stood. "Would you like another cracker?"

Billie stared at her for a long moment before the question made any sense. She shook her head.

"Good. Then we're done talking. You sit here and bleed. I'll be back in a few hours to collect the product."

"Wait," Billie pleaded, but Kaitlyn did not.

Caleb didn't usually go out drinking with the guys from the quarry after work. Then again, he was usually in a hurry to get home so he could see Billie in that narrow window they had together before she had to run off to the Silver Coin to be his dad's servant and spy. But she was still out of town, and still hadn't responded to his texts or calls, so why the hell not?

At Fred's Bar and Grill, Joaquin regaled him with tales of his recent date with a girl from Evergreen. Brock was there, too, his cast propped up on a chair, a beer in his hand, surely on painkillers he was not supposed to be drinking with. Caleb's leg still felt good, though he affected a limp to avoid questions about how he had healed so fast. Caleb kept the onyx in his pocket, and it continued to dull the vibrations around him. The alcohol did too, which was both a comfort and a concern. Even with the vibrations dulled, he could still sense the turquoise in Joaquin's hatband, the diamonds in the wedding band that Brock wore.

Light shined into the dim room as the door opened, and Caleb turned to see Chloe and Luke enter. Luke wore sandals with socks and knee-length shorts that exposed pale, chubby, hairy legs. He had on a Broncos jersey and a backward baseball cap. And Chloe was just as gorgeous as ever in tight jeans with embroidered flowers on the pockets and a pink spaghetti strap tank top. She squealed when she saw him and threw her arms around his neck. Caleb squeezed back maybe a second longer than he should have, then shook hands with Luke and moved over one barstool to make room for both of them.

Of course he was hoping to talk to Chloe, but she took the farther seat and immediately started chatting with the bartender, leaving Caleb stuck next to Luke. Caleb nodded to the beer glass the bartender slid over to him. "Which one you trying?" Fred's had an extensive menu of odd and interesting craft beers.

"Huh? Oh, it's Coors Light."

"Coors… man, you've got to try one of the craft beers next round."

"Nah, I like this one."

Caleb shrugged. "Your loss."

Luke talked about the game that was playing on the TV over the bar, but after a while, Caleb finally said, "Sorry, I think baseball's boring as shit."

"Any more rabid marmots in town?" Luke asked after an awkward moment.

"Any what?" Then Caleb realized he must be referring to the Scarlet-infected animals, like the one he and Chloe had encountered the day before. Reverend Provine had also papered the town with warning flyers, advertising a mass prayer session happening at the church tomorrow and advising people not to shoot the demon animals. "Uh, it was a beaver that Chloe and I saw. And it wasn't rabid, it was like that deer out at your place."

"I never knew rabies could be that bad," Luke said.

"It's not—"

Caleb's phone buzzed and he gladly took the excuse to break away from Luke. He looked at the number. It was local, but not anyone he had in his contacts. He would be happy to talk to a car warranty salesman if it meant he didn't have to waste one more braincell trying to be friendly to Luke.

"Hello?" He put a hand to his other ear and headed toward the exit.

"Hi, is this Caleb Mulligan?" a raspy female voice asked.

"It is."

"This is Kim, from the Silver Coin Hotel."

"Yeah, hi, Kim. How are you? I just saw your wife yesterday."

Kim was married to Heather, the owner of the Enchanted Mountain Metaphysical Shop. They'd been together as long as Caleb had lived in Juniper.

"Yes, she told me," Kim said with a mischievous lilt to her tone. Caleb winced. Billie was going to come back to all kinds of rumors about what he'd been up to in her absence. "Unfortunately, I have some bad news."

"Uh oh." He was outside now, away from the noise of the bar.

With Billie out of town, that meant the news had to be about his dad.

"It's your dad," Kim confirmed. "He… well, he got attacked by an animal. He's okay, though," she quickly corrected. "Not like those mountain lion attacks a couple of weeks ago. Nothing like that."

"Okay," Caleb said. "What kind of animal?"

"We're not really sure. It happened two days ago, down by the lake. He says it was a deer, but I don't know, that's pretty unusual. Anyway, he's back from the hospital now, and I just realized that no one let you know about it."

"He's okay, though?"

"Relatively. He'll be bedridden for a couple of days."

"If he'll stay put."

Kim snort-laughed. "I give that a couple of hours."

"Thanks, Kim."

"You're welcome. Take care."

Caleb hung up and stood there tapping his phone against his palm. Had it been the same deer that had torn up Chloe and Luke's U-Haul? But why would it have attacked him? Mitch knew what Scarlet did to people, so Caleb couldn't imagine his dad would be so reckless as to take Scarlet himself.

Chloe stepped outside and said his name. Caleb shoved his phone into his pocket and looked down at her.

"Is everything okay?" she asked.

"My dad. He got attacked by one of those animals."

Her hands flew to her mouth.

"He's fine," Caleb said. "But I feel like I should go see him." He hadn't even realized he was going to say it, but once it was out, he knew he needed to. He and his dad had a lot of unresolved issues, but when Caleb had been in the hospital after being attacked, Mitch had been right there at his bedside nearly the whole time.

"Do you need a ride?" Chloe asked.

"No, it's just over at the Silver Coin."

She put a hand up, and said, "Let me rephrase that. You've been drinking. You need a ride."

He gestured toward the brown bottle in her hand, and she held it up to display the root beer label. "I don't drink much alcohol. Makes things… too fuzzy for me. Like I might not be able to use my powers if I needed to."

Billie had once told him something similar, that drinking made her feel like she wouldn't be able to shift if she needed to. Caleb shrugged. He hadn't had enough alcohol to need a designated driver, but it would be nice to not have to face his dad alone. Maybe Chloe could do some of her healing on him, like she'd done for Caleb.

"Okay," he said. "Let's go."

She swigged her root beer and went back into the bar to retrieve Luke. Caleb would have preferred to leave him here, but he couldn't really protest.

It only took a few minutes to drive to the Silver Coin. As Chloe pulled into the parking garage, Caleb said, "He's probably in his room, but if not, we can check the casino."

"Casino?" Luke asked.

Whoops. Guess the newcomers hadn't yet been trusted to join his dad's illicit games on the top floor of the hotel.

"Just a nickname for his office," he covered. "You'll see." Caleb was torn about whether to expose the secret. They lived in Juniper now. They'd have to find out eventually.

Fortunately, Mitch was in his suite on the third floor, the large one right next to where Caleb's old room had been. The door was propped open with a wedge doorstopper. Caleb knocked on the door and Mitch shouted, "Enter!" The TV blared with his favorite crime show, but Mitch paused it as soon as the three of them walked in.

"Well look who finally decided to pay his old pop a visit." He was propped up by a dozen pillows on the bed.

"Could have told me you were injured, you know," Caleb said.

"Nah, you're busy. Besides—" Mitch gestured toward his

bandaged arm with the healthy one. "This is nothing but a chicken scratch. Everyone's overreacting. I ain't dead yet."

"He has more than a bum mit," said another voice, and Reno Bridges materialized in the corner of the room. Chloe jumped, then put a hand over her heart.

Reno had been haunting the Silver Coin since the 1920s, when a fight in the dance hall had ended with a knife in his side. He could manifest in a couple of different forms. Today, he wore a tipped fedora and pinstripe suit; the type of real gangster Mitch wished he was.

"That young nurse who was here earlier said the wounds on his chest were quite serious," the ghost said.

"Thanks, Uncle Reno," Caleb said. "I know he never tells me the whole truth."

There was no blood relation between Caleb and the ghost, but he'd gotten in the habit of calling him Uncle during his teenage years when he'd lived in the hotel and the ghost had sometimes been around a lot more than his dad was.

Mitch grunted and glanced at the corner where Reno sat. "Talking to your ghost again, are you? Thought you'd grow out of that game. Guess it would mean growing up in general, though."

Caleb didn't take the bait. This kind of thing hardly even made him mad anymore, it was just a part of their script. When he didn't react, Mitch appeared to notice the other two in the room for the first time. He pointed a finger gun at them and said, "Mr. and Mrs. Nolting, if I remember right?"

Chloe looked surprised. "Sieben-Nolting for me, sir," she said. Luke stepped forward to extend a handshake.

"I try to remember everyone who stays in my hotel. You decided to become locals, didn't you? How are you liking it?"

While Mitch and Luke chatted, Reno swooped off the chair in the corner and swirled around Chloe in a gust of cool air. "My, you are a pretty peach, aren't you?" He manifested again, standing in front of her.

Chloe squeaked, but she looked delighted rather than fearful. "Wow, you are a far more substantial spirit than I've ever met before."

Reno bowed theatrically, the edges of his ghostly body fading and trailing a second behind his movements. "Renaldo Bridges, at your service, miss."

He extended a ghostly hand and Chloe reached out to take it. He lowered his lips to her hand and she giggled.

"That is *really* cold."

Reno did a funky little dance step and elbowed Caleb in the side, which felt like a puff of cold air. "Careful with this one, or you'll end up like me."

"No, it's not like that—" Caleb said. And then he realized that both Mitch and Luke were gawking at them.

"Chloe?" Luke said, a little scared quaver to his voice. "Who are you talking to?"

"Reno Bridges," she said. "He's right here…" But as she gestured toward the ghost, he faded into the dusty sunbeams shining through the window and disappeared. "He *was* right here," she corrected.

"They're just yanking our chain," Mitch said.

Caleb and Chloe glanced at each other, and tacitly agreed to let it go, at least for the time being.

"So," Caleb said. "How'd you get in a fight with a deer, anyway?"

Mitch grunted. "That was no ordinary deer."

"Bloody looking fur, face falling half off, red eyes?" Caleb said.

"Oh, so you've met," Mitch said.

"Might have been the same one that attacked their U-Haul." Caleb shook his head. "But I thought we'd figured out these monsters only went after Scarlet? So why'd it go after you?"

Mitch's eyes flicked to the newcomers.

"They know what the Scarlet does," Caleb said.

"We were at the Fourth of July party," Chloe confirmed. "When that… creature charged through.”

"I thought that was a stunt to promote some horror movie?" Luke said.

Chloe smiled placatingly at him. "No, honey, it was like that deer that attacked our moving truck."

"That was rabies?"

"It's not rabies," she said patiently.

"Why'd it attack their U-Haul?" Mitch asked, shifting his eyes suspiciously between Chloe and Luke.

"Joaquin was there," Caleb said.

"Ah." That needed no more explanation. Mitch shrugged and then winced as the movement stretched his bandages. "Not sure. The thing just charged out of the forest at me. I'd been taking a swim."

Caleb groaned. "The lake water's contaminated." He explained about dropping the vial into the lake, and about Mouse tossing the whole tray into the river.

"We're all fucked, then," Mitch proclaimed once Caleb was finished. "If those things keep transforming…"

"Could make it a new tourist draw," Caleb said. "Visit Juniper and hunt the demon deer."

It was a joke, but Mitch glared daggers at him. You didn't joke about tourism with Mitch—it was his whole livelihood, his sworn life's purpose.

"I want you to find Elliot Moran and bring him to talk to me."

"Me?" Caleb said.

"Yes, *son*, you. I'd send Billie, but she's still off on her *Eat, Pray, Love* journey to find herself, isn't she?"

Caleb hated to hear Mitch talk about Billie like that, but he wasn't going to let his dad get to him. He *wasn't*. "What's Elliot Moran got to do with anything?"

"He's the one bringing that shit into town. Maybe he knows what it's made of."

"Maybe he knows of an antidote?" Chloe supplied.

Mitch made a finger gun gesture at her, clicking his tongue.

"I'm not one of your goons," Caleb said.

"No, you're not. You going to let this town be overrun with demon animals just to spite your dear old dad?"

It was tempting. But Caleb stood up and said, "I'll see if I can find him."

Luke looked up from his phone and swiped some game off the screen. "Uh, good to see you, Mr. Mulligan. Hope you're better soon! Make sure the nurse gives you that rabies shot."

Caleb resisted the urge to punch Luke in the eye. Had he not heard a word of that entire conversation? Chloe and Luke followed Caleb out into the hallway. The TV turned on full blast before they were out the door.

"Where to now?" Chloe asked, sounding eager to continue their adventure.

"Eh, just back to Fred's," Caleb said.

"But what about… was it Elliot?"

"Yeah, I'll text him. I'm not gonna go banging down his door."

The truth was that Elliot Moran was a sketchy dude, and Caleb didn't want Chloe anywhere near him. Or dumbass Luke either, for that matter.

"You're sure?"

"I'm sure. Let me buy you another root beer."

She looked worried, but nodded. As they reached the parking garage, Chloe suddenly balked.

"What is it?" Caleb looked around, sure she'd spotted another infected animal about to rush toward them. But she wasn't looking at anything in particular. Her eyes were unfocused, staring off into nothing. Caleb touched her arm. "Chloe, are you okay?" The lowkey vibrations he always picked up from the stones on her bracelet were practically making the air buzz around her.

"Shh," she hissed, and shook him off of her arm. Caleb looked at Luke, but he was on his phone again, oblivious to whatever was happening. Chloe stared into space for a moment longer, then squinted in confusion. "I... I have to make a phone call." She pulled her phone out and walked toward the parking garage entrance. Caleb followed, giving her space, but staying close enough he could hear what she said. She paced for a moment, then said, "Hey, Aunt Lisa. I know you're probably at work, but you remember that cute little clothing shop downtown you took me to? With all the shawls and those bottle cap earrings? So... I was getting *really* strong messages about that place just now. No idea what that's about, but I thought you might know. Call me back when you get the chance."

"What was that about?" Caleb asked when she returned to the car.

"Oh, nothing. I'm sure it's nothing," she said, but she seemed rattled, and remained distracted and distant the rest of the evening.

THURSDAY

Time became meaningless in the underground dark room. It could have been night or day; she might have been there for an hour or a week. The blood draining zapped her energy, leaving her constantly lightheaded and with a chill in her limbs. She screamed for help until her voice went raw, but the sound only echoed against the stone walls. Noises leaked in sometimes from overhead: the rumble of a large vehicle, a clank as someone stepped on the manhole cover in the sidewalk. She recalled the ghost tour, the reports that employees of the clothing shop had heard strange sounds, seen objects moved. Any sounds she made down here would just add to that ghost story. She'd come full circle, in a way, from telling ghost stories at the Silver Coin that covered for noises from the casino.

These walls are my cage, the ghost of Reno Bridges had said. If she died, would she end up haunting this awful little basement for eternity?

As time drifted, a memory resurfaced that Billie hadn't thought of in a long time. It was one of the many fights between her parents, about a planned school field trip to the Denver zoo. They needed to sign the permission form in order for Billie to be allowed to ride the bus out of town with the rest of her class, but her mother had been firmly opposed. In a misguided attempt to persuade her, Billie's dad had said something like, "If you were a lonely tiger, wouldn't you want visitors?"

"I would rather die than be held captive like that."

Her dad had argued that zoos were humane and conservation focused and that she was being unreasonable, but she remained vehement, and Billie never had gone to the zoo with the rest of her class, that year or any other.

"I'd rather die…" she whispered to herself as she tugged on the restraints around her wrists, trying to decide if the sentiment was as true for herself as it had been for her mother. Wondering if it would be true for the other shifters in nearby rooms. Was there freedom in death, or was it only a different sort of cage?

Kaitlyn didn't return, nor did Elliot Moran, but another man appeared once. He had a shaved head, broad shoulders, and a hard, chiseled jaw—maybe the cop that Travis had mentioned. He sprayed her with more of that chemical that kept her from shifting, made her eat more graham crackers and drink water, and forced her to chew some chalky vitamins. So she'd keep producing more blood, Billie assumed. More Scarlet. He carried the blood bag out with him, having replaced it with another one.

Her mother had told her many times that they couldn't ever tell anyone about their shapeshifting because people who couldn't do it would be jealous. Had her mother's family found themselves in a situation like this? Maybe she had been the only one to escape. Billie had guarded her secret, though not as closely as she could have, and here she was. Trapped. Caged. The others were nearby, trapped just like her. She pretended she could feel their presence, just on the other side of the stone wall. Shared suffering, each of them in their own isolated space.

The next time the door opened, Billie didn't even look up to see which of her kidnappers it was. She closed her eyes and braced for the chemical spray. It still lingered in the air from last time. Travis had managed to shift and escape, so they surely wouldn't make the mistake of allowing it to wear off again.

"Billie." The voice was a whisper—a woman's voice, but not Kaitlyn's clipped, formal tones. The zip tie around her right wrist snapped, freeing her arm. Billie forced herself to open her eyes.

She didn't recognize the woman at first: middle-aged with light lines around her eyes and dyed blonde hair, wearing a short-sleeved flannel shirt and jeans.

"Come on, hurry up, we can get you out of here," she whispered as she cut the last of the zip ties.

"Lisa?"

"Yes, of course, hon." She expertly detached the needle from Billie's arm. "Can you walk?"

Billie stood on numb feet, her head swimming. She put her palm to her temple and nodded.

"The others," she said as she stumbled away from the awful chair. "We have to help the others escape too."

"Do you know where they are?"

Billie took one more look around the dark room. There was a sealed manhole in the ceiling, and the door that Lisa was urging her toward. She'd observed no passageways that might lead to other rooms. The ghost tour guide had said these were coal storage rooms, not tunnels. Reluctantly, she shook her head.

"Let's get you safe first, and then we'll find the others, I promise."

"Don't make promises," Billie said.

Lisa pulled open a creaking door and Billie followed her up a narrow staircase. At the top, she told Billie to wait while she peered around a corner, and then waved for her to come along. They passed through a storage area full of cardboard boxes and mannequins and racks of clothes. Lisa pressed the bar on a metal door that opened into a hallway, littered with an overflow of storage from the shops. They hurried down it, then out a second door. Her dad's truck was parked on the street, but he wasn't in it. Lisa hurried around to the driver's side and started the engine. Billie opened the door, hesitating before she climbed inside. Was this actually a rescue, or some new ruse? She didn't know Lisa, had no reason to trust her.

"Where's Dad?" she asked.

Instead of answering, Lisa pounded on the car horn. Billie jumped, but her skin didn't ripple. Still too much of the chemical in her blood for that instinct to surface.

"He's standing guard," Lisa said. "Come on, hurry up."

Billie didn't trust her, but a second later, her dad hurried around the corner toward them. She got in the truck and he hopped in right behind her, slamming the door. Billie scooted over to the middle, stuck between them. Lisa navigated quickly out of the downtown area.

Billie's dad put his hands on Billie's cheeks and kissed her forehead. She squirmed away from his touch, so intrusive and unwanted it made her stomach flip. He let go and said, "What did they *do* to you, baby doll?"

In answer, she held up her arm, where a piece of medical tape still flapped. Her inner elbow was bruised and blood caked around the insertion point.

"Scarlet," she explained. "It's made from shifter blood."

Lisa and her dad looked at each other, something silent passing between them.

"How did you find me?" Billie asked.

"Mmm," Lisa said. "Let's just say I had a feeling."

"You have a *feeling* about where all the others are being kept?" Lisa shook her head. *Of course not.* Billie put her still aching head in her hands. Had Travis and Samantha managed to escape, or had they been caught after Billie was tranquilized? "Uh?" Billie looked up as Lisa pulled the truck onto a highway that crossed over the river, driving away from every part of this new place that she recognized. "Where the hell are we going?"

"Home," Lisa said.

"But the Lesniks… they're still all down there!" Billie was on the verge of a panic attack now, feeling just as caged and trapped in the middle seat of this small truck as she had in the stone basement.

"We have a plan," her dad said.

They were leaving Durango, driving through territory Billie hadn't seen before. She tried to recall what turns they'd already taken since leaving downtown, and memorize landmarks they passed on the way, so that if she had to go back to Durango by herself she could remember the way. Because she didn't trust that Lisa and her dad *would* go back to rescue the others.

The text Caleb sent Elliot got a delayed response of, "Sorry, out of town." Caleb planned to stop by Elliot's parents' house after work just to make sure, but he wasn't going to push. He wasn't one of his dad's goons, and he wasn't going to let this situation draw him into his dad's pseudo mafia delusion.

But the day didn't exactly go the way Caleb expected. Everyone was sent home from the quarry early because red-eyed birds kept dive-bombing the workers. Joaquin got everyone worked up, telling them about the deer in the U-Haul and the beaver downtown. The other guys were on the verge of getting their guns and plunging into the forest in a free-for-all hunt, but Joaquin had apparently been fully convinced by Reverend Provine's theory that shooting the animals would simply cause the demons inside to jump to another host. He rallied several of the others, and the group all went to the church. Caleb declined to join the mob, and started back toward the cabin.

Halfway there, his phone started to buzz. Thinking—hoping—it might be Billie, he reached for it, but saw Brock's picture on the screen instead. When he answered, Brock was crying and cursing and making no damn sense. So Caleb changed course and drove up to Brock's place. Even though Caleb had hung up a mile ago, Brock was standing in the driveway with the phone still to his ear. He'd dropped his crutches in the middle of the driveway and was just standing on one foot like a confused flamingo. Caleb parked the car and opened the door.

"What the hell are you doing out here?" he yelled at Brock.

But then he saw. Body parts were strewn across the yard and driveway. Caleb lifted his boot and grimaced. He'd stepped on a bloody human ear. A mutated squirrel crouched on a stump, gnawing on what appeared to be a finger with a blue painted nail. Other chunks of flesh were spread around like the aftermath of a bear attacking a dumpster.

"Oh, shit," Caleb said.

When Brock's wife, Tara, had been attacked by the Scarlet Monster, Brock had been so distraught that he'd asked Caleb to help him bury her right there, rather than face the police and give impossible-sounding answers to their inevitable questions. Brock had been afraid that no one would believe what they'd seen, that he would be accused of her murder. Caleb had known it was a bad idea to bury her, but he'd done it anyway, to help his friend. But now, with the forest swarming with Scarlet-drunk animals, some of them must have smelled the Scarlet in Tara's blood and gone after her buried body.

A bear came snuffling up the driveway. Or what used to be a bear. It had no fur left, just exposed red muscle and teeth so elongated it practically looked saber toothed.

"Get in the car," Caleb said. When Brock didn't move, Caleb went over and roughly grabbed his friend's arm. Brock hobbled toward the car, leaning awkwardly and heavily against Caleb.

Caleb snatched the crutches from the ground and stuffed them into the back seat. Just as he shut the car door, the bear went right for those chunks of flesh that were strewn across the driveway. The squirrel dropped the finger it had been gnawing on and leaped at the bear. The bear roared, batting at the squirrel, who hung on to the bear's back, chomping at the bear's fur over and over. Caleb reversed out of the driveway, leaving the horror show behind.

"I'm going to take you over to your mom's place, okay?"

Brock said nothing, just watched a rabbit on the side of the road, standing upright like a creepy cartoon, red eyes following the car as it passed by.

"They're everywhere," Brock said.

And indeed, they were. Caleb intercepted Brock's mom at the base of her driveway—she was on her way to the church, and Brock switched cars, agreeing to go with her. On the drive back to the cabin, Caleb saw more birds like those at the quarry squabbling between each other. A racoon that had lost all the fur on its head climbed on top of a car on Miners Avenue and screamed at the driver inside, who swatted at it with a handful of tourist brochures. The whole town was overrun with mutated animals.

Inside the cabin, Caleb packed a duffle bag. Then he sat in the car out front, tapping his thumbs on the steering wheel. It was about a two-hour drive into Denver. He had friends there, and some family on his mom's side. He could stay with them, find a new job, and leave this whole mess behind. That's what he'd wanted. That's what he'd been trying to get Billie to agree to back when she thought she couldn't leave Juniper. Hell, if Billie had found some of her family down in Durango, like she'd been hoping to, maybe that's where they could start a new life together. If she ever bothered to call him back, they could negotiate that. *He* was getting out of Juniper, at any rate.

And yet, he couldn't bring himself to start the car and actually leave.

A moose clomped down the center of the abandoned street. Its massive torso was twisted, misshapen, and nearly all the fur had sloughed off, exposing the bright red muscle beneath. Caleb swore its antlers had changed, too, sharpened into knife-like tips more like an elk, and—*oh, god, are those...?*—yes, on the creature's back, the nubs of wings. Just like Daniel Gadbury had developed.

The moose sauntered past Caleb's car, hardly acknowledging him. Caleb held his breath. Then, as if attracted by a sudden sound, the moose lifted its head and stared down the street. An owl divebombed the moose, swiping a chunk from its torso. It dove a second time, and the moose swung its head and knocked the bird down, then stepped on it, crushing it to a mass of blood and feathers with its massive hoof. And then proceeded to tear off chunks of the dead owl and eat them.

"Jesus," Caleb breathed. He pulled the onyx out of his pocket and clenched it, and instantly felt calmer, more focused. He opened his hand and stared at the stone. There really was something to this earth magic he'd been experiencing. Chloe had said she could help him learn to control his newly awakened powers, maybe even do something with it other than just be overwhelmed by vibrations all the time. If he left Juniper, what were the chances he'd find someone else who could teach him?

He waited until the moose finished consuming the owl and wandered a little farther down the street. Then he pulled his phone out.

Town's kinda on lockdown, he texted to Chloe. ***I don't really want to stay by myself. Could I hole up with you guys for a little while?***

The response was almost instantaneous. ***Yes!!!*** And an emoji with hearts for eyes. Caleb couldn't help but grin.

He started the car, waiting to see if the sound of the engine attracted the moose. It didn't. He turned a street early so he wouldn't risk passing it, and drove up to Chloe's house.

Luke answered the door. "Hey, man," Caleb said. "Hope this isn't awkward…"

"Dude, everything's got rabies, it's like a zombie apocalypse out there," Luke said, and ushered Caleb inside. "Besides, Chloe made way too much food."

Chloe held up flour-covered hands and came over to kiss Caleb on the cheek, a greeting he had not been expecting. "I bake when I'm stressed," she admitted. "Cookie?"

Caleb tossed his bag on an empty kitchen chair and seized a cookie from one of the baking sheets on the table. "Wow," he said after the first bite. "That's *really* good."

"Right?" Luke said. "Pure magic." He winked at Chloe, who rolled her eyes. Luke grabbed another cookie and then hooked a thumb toward the living room. "Game's on, wanna watch?"

"I'll catch up in a minute," Caleb said.

Luke shrugged and headed to the couch, trailing cookie crumbs.

When Caleb thought he was probably out of earshot, he said to Chloe, "He doesn't really believe in your powers, does he?"

"Hmm?" Chloe looked up from the bowl she was stirring. "Oh, he just doesn't understand. Kind of rationalizes things away. Most people do."

"He couldn't see the ghost either."

"No, but he *does* believe in those. Sometimes he sees orbs. Especially in the pictures we take on ghost tours."

"Orbs," Caleb said skeptically. "You mean flecks of dust on the camera lens?"

"Hey, now," she said, a little defensively, but her face remained playful and relaxed. "You don't know that's all they are."

"Fair enough." Caleb couldn't just dismiss anything anymore, not after what he'd seen and experienced. "So only people who have some type of supernatural ability can actually see ghosts?"

Chloe shrugged. "You know, I think you might be onto something. Billie can definitely see them too."

"For sure," Caleb said, before he realized the implications of admitting that.

Chloe raised an eyebrow at him. "So she has something going on?"

"I... think I have to let her decide whether to tell you that."

Chloe winked at him. "I get it. Do you bake?"

The change of topic caught him a little off-guard. "Me? Nah. Mom always chased me out of the kitchen."

"How about Billie?"

Caleb almost snorted. "Uh, no. Billie has a lot of skills, but cooking and cleaning are not exactly at the top of the list."

"She strikes me as more of a wildcat," Chloe said.

Caleb considered her. Had she guessed about Billie's shapeshifting? Why would she use that term, if she didn't?

"You could say that," Caleb said. Why did she keep bringing up Billie? "Hey, I don't have to stay here if it's going to be weird."

"Don't be silly." Chloe washed her hands and dried them on a pink towel. "It's awful out there. I watched a little orange kitten throw itself at an elk like it was a big old piece of walking catnip."

"Probably not the peaceful idyllic mountain life you were looking for."

Caleb said it flippantly, but to his horror, Chloe suddenly burst into tears. He started to his feet and reached to comfort her, looking over his shoulder to see where Luke was, but he didn't seem to notice his wife sobbing in the kitchen. Caleb guided her into a chair and rubbed his hand over her back.

"Hey, I'm sorry," he said.

"No." She sniffled. "It's just, you're *right*. You're exactly right." She wiped her hand over her face, then realized she'd smeared flour all over herself. Caleb pulled the towel from the oven handle and wet a corner of it. "Did you ever get ahold of that guy?" Chloe asked after she wiped her face and hands with the towel.

"Who? Elliot? Uh, no, he's out of town and wouldn't call me back."

Chloe sighed. "He was the only one who might know a cure. So we just have to rot up here until those things eat us alive."

"Nothing's eating you alive," Caleb said, even as the memory of the Scarlet Monster racing after Tara replayed in his mind. He *wasn't* going to let that happen to Chloe. "We just have to stay safe in here, and eventually they'll all kill each other off. And that's awful, but we'll wait it out and everything will be okay again soon."

"Wait it out," Chloe repeated. Then the oven timer dinged and she hopped up, absorbed in the baking again.

Lisa lived in a well-maintained mobile home that was full of houseplants and decorative fantasy-style artwork: crystal dragons and ceramic gnomes and fairy windchimes. The town, Mancos, was about half an hour from Durango, and seemed to be more the size of Juniper, from what Billie had been able to see on their drive in.

Billie's backpack was already on Lisa's couch, and her dad's bag lay half unpacked on the floor of the bedroom. Proof that he had spent a night or two here. Had they been in bed together when Kaitlyn and Elliot showed up at the Lesniks' house? He should have been there, with Billie. He should have been there to protect her. She grabbed the backpack, trying to halt that thought spiral. Lisa had rescued her; she should be grateful to her. She *was* grateful to her. Why should Billie care what kind of relationship Lisa had with her dad? It was childish.

She yanked the zipper open and searched for her toothbrush and clean clothes. She definitely hadn't brought enough. Her hairbrush was missing, forgotten on the sink at the motel, probably. And she still had no shoes; those had been left on the Lesniks' living room floor. She dug around for her phone before remembering that had also been abandoned at the Lesniks' house.

"Let me bandage your arm," Lisa said.

Billie glanced at the tape hanging onto the skin of her inner arm, which she'd practically forgotten was there. She wadded up the clothes she'd grabbed, holding them in her lap as she sat in the kitchen chair. Lisa swabbed the insertion point with alcohol and deftly wrapped some gauze around her arm. Probably, she'd been a nurse of some type before she was a saloon call-girl, but Billie didn't care enough to ask.

Once the bandage was secured, Lisa kept her hand on Billie's arm, her eyes closed. Billie yanked her arm away and stood. Lisa looked surprised, and perhaps a little hurt.

"Baby doll," her dad said from the couch, "She can take some of the pain away."

Billie wasn't interested in indulging whatever Reiki or healing touch powers Lisa thought she had.

"No," she said. "I need this pain."

She slammed the bathroom door and turned on the shower. Listening to the water run, she leaned against the sink. Everything from the last few days hit all at once, crashing through her like a wave. She was lashing out at the wrong person, she knew. She had a tendency to do that, try to blame all her pain on someone else. It had been so easy to put her dad in that role for so long. Lisa had helped her and never hurt her. But after the things she'd been through, how could she ever trust anyone? Just because someone hadn't hurt her yet didn't mean they never would.

Billie peeled her clothes off and ran her hands across her human skin, holding herself like she rarely let anyone else hold her. She stepped into the shower and let the water run until the tears wouldn't come anymore and she felt wrung dry on the inside, even as she soaked on the outside. The gauze Lisa had just put on soaked through and she unwrapped it, watching the blood—her special, dangerous blood—swirl down the drain along with the water.

Clean, and tired, and somewhat numb, she finally emerged from the bathroom. She'd taken a long time putting her wet hair into a French Braid that she tied with a purple band she found in the cabinet above the sink. Her arm no longer bled, but she'd found a bandage to put over the bruise anyway.

The whole house smelled like fresh cut tomatoes and spicy sausage. Her stomach rumbled at the smell of it, but bile also rose at the memory of her kidnappers forcing her to eat. She may never be able to eat a graham cracker again, after... how long had she been in that basement?

"There she is!" Lisa said brightly.

"How long was I in there?" Billie asked.

"Long enough we were about to send a search party," Lisa said.

The flippant tone confused Billie until she realized Lisa was referring to how long she'd spent in the shower.

"No," Billie said. "I mean, how long was I... captured? What day is it?"

"Oh," Lisa said. "Gosh. Uh, it's Thursday. It was yesterday night we realized you were missing."

Kaitlyn had stormed the Lesniks' house on Wednesday morning. Just over a day, then.

"You're safe now, baby doll." Billie turned to see her dad on the couch, his feet propped up on the coffee table.

"But the others..." Billie protested. "They're probably still down there..."

"It's okay," her dad said. "It's taken care of."

"What?" Billie said. "By who?"

"The cops," Lisa said.

"Excuse me?" Billie rounded on her, anger rising and burning away the decision she'd made to be nicer to Lisa. "The *cops*? You know the cops are in on it, right?"

Lisa held out a plate of spaghetti like a peace offering. Billie stared at it for a second and then took the plate and sat at the small round table, in the same chair where Lisa had bandaged her arm. Lisa set another plate down and Billie's dad joined them.

"Not *all* of them are in on it," Lisa said.

While they ate, Lisa and Billie's dad recounted the adventures they'd had over the last two days. He and Lisa had also, somehow, puzzled out that Scarlet was involved, and Lisa had contacted some distant cousin who was a DEA agent. A raid was going to happen on the underground rooms in the next day or so. The two of them took it upon themselves to rescue Billie, though, rather than let her suffer any longer than she had to, once Lisa had her "feeling" about which one Billie was being kept in.

"I thought Scarlet wasn't actually illegal?" Billie asked.

"Apparently an executive order went through last week that listed it as a controlled substance," her dad said. "They can push these things through pretty fast when they're motivated."

Billie chewed her spaghetti in silence, hardly even tasting it. Since shifter blood was the key ingredient in Scarlet, making Scarlet illegal could have some seriously negative impacts for her kind. She'd certainly think twice before going to a hospital if she was hurt. When she'd tried to donate blood when Caleb needed it, they'd simply turned her away, saying they detected Scarlet. What would happen now if they understood that her blood *was* Scarlet?

"In any case, you're free now, and it will all be over for the others soon."

"I'm free now," Billie repeated. She looked between Lisa and her dad, sorting through the layers of emotion, trying to bring the gratitude forward. It was there, and she sat with it, letting it shine brighter than all the fear and distrust and anger and sadness surrounding it. She *was* free, for now. "Thank you," she whispered.

Lisa placed her hand on Billie's arm and smiled at her, and this time Billie let it stay for a moment before she pulled back. And somehow, she did feel a little better. Lisa didn't act offended this time when Billie pulled away, but she wrapped her hand around a tiger's eye pendant that hung around her neck, before returning to her food.

By the time they finished eating, the weakness and lightheadedness from the blood draining had mostly faded. Lisa and her dad tried to distract her by watching a lighthearted comedy movie that Billie hardly paid attention to. How could she sit here and pretend things were normal when Travis and Samantha were probably hiding in the forest? When the rest of their family were still being drained and tortured?

Around ten that night, her dad and Lisa went into Lisa's room together, having made a big fuss of positioning pillows and blankets on the couch to make Billie the most comfortable makeshift bed possible. But Billie had no intention of sleeping in it. She sat cross-legged on the nest of blankets, listening to every sound, as attentive as her human senses allowed.

A while after the bedroom door closed, Billie slid on a pair of Lisa's shoes that had been left by the door, plain white tennis shoes that were almost the right size. When they first came in, she had watched Lisa hang the truck keys on a flower-shaped key rack beside the door. She wrapped her fist tightly around the keys, to keep them from jingling, and eased the deadbolt open. The door creaked and she paused, but the bedroom door remained shut, no sounds from inside except her dad's bubbly snore.

She stepped outside and eased the door closed, wincing at the creak in that same sticky spot. What she assumed was Lisa's Subaru was parked on the street in front, and her dad's truck was under the carport. She put the truck in neutral, left the driver's side door open, and let it roll backward out of the carport.

Once the truck was out of the driveway, then she slammed the door shut, started the engine and took off as quickly as she could. If she could get at least partway to Durango before they knew she was gone, then it would be harder for them to catch up with her. She glanced at the gas gauge—half a tank. Plenty to get her there, and possibly back. On the long, straight highway, Billie drove as fast as the rickety little truck would go.

She retraced the roads they'd driven and found downtown, bright with streetlights but almost entirely vacant. She parked at the end of the block that had the underground rooms. With the truck turned off, she manually rolled down the window and sniffed the air. That faint scent of Scarlet she'd noticed before still lingered on the wind. It was, she knew now, the scent of her own blood, the blood of others like herself. She couldn't believe she hadn't made the connection before.

She slouched in her seat, trying to position herself where she could see as much of the block as possible, but so that someone passing by might miss that she was in there. Lisa and her dad were confident that the DEA were going to raid the underground rooms and free the other shifters, but Billie didn't trust that. Even if they did, how much worse would the world become for people like her if the police who raided and the media who reported on it exposed the existence of her kind? How much more suffering would come once others understood the power of shifter blood?

FRIDAY

No one had driven past or walked down this block for nearly half an hour. A little after midnight, Billie dug a crowbar out of her dad's tool chest and yanked on every sidewalk manhole cover on the block, but they were all sealed shut.

A white van drove past with its lights off. Billie pressed herself into the recessed doorway of the clothing shop just in time to avoid being seen. From the shadows, she heard the engine shut off, and the quiet click of a door shutting. As quietly as she could, and staying in human form with the crowbar clutched in her hands, she slunk toward the end of the block. She hadn't shifted yet since Lisa rescued her, though she was pretty sure the effects of the spray had long ago worn off. She could run if she needed to. Or attack.

She peered around the corner of the brick building. The van was parked close to the doorway that Lisa had led Billie out of, which she knew led to the building's back hallway. Her dad's truck was parked on the other side of the street, further down. Billie moved a step closer to the van, shifting only her eyes to see better in the dark. It worked, painlessly, and the night landscape transformed. The driver's seat of the van was empty. No getaway driver, then.

Billie was tentatively reaching toward the back door of the van when the building's door opened. She darted into the alleyway, hiding behind a dumpster. Three figures appeared, one of them large and stumbling, head hanging low and back rounded. The other two shoved him into the van and reappeared a moment later, slamming the door behind them and heading back to the building. Billie's heart pounded. If the cop involved had gotten wind of the planned raid, they'd be moving shop now before anything could be discovered. The second they disappeared inside, she raced over and flung open the van's back door.

The man startled. Even in the dark, she could recognize him from all of those photos she'd seen in the Lesniks' house. This was definitely Stan. "Who the hell are you?" he bellowed.

No time to explain. Billie moved into the shaft of light from the streetlight and shifted only her eyes, letting them go as cat-like as she could without folding her entire face.

"I'm like you," she said. "And I'm going to get you out of here."

His eyes went wide and he gave a grunt of assent. His arm was zip tied to a rung on the van's wall. Billie glanced around for a tool she might use to cut him free, but of course nothing like that was left just laying around here. She'd abandoned the crowbar on the ground in the alleyway, and it wouldn't have helped here in any case. In her survey of the van's interior, she noticed two aerosol cans laying on their sides near Stan's feet—that awful spray that prevented shifting. She couldn't smell it in the air, though. Maybe Stan hadn't been sprayed recently?

No tools in sight, but she did have teeth. Billie let her face shift enough to draw out sharp canines. Just as she started to lean toward the zip ties around Stan's bulky wrists, she heard the building's door open again.

"I'm going to get you out of here," she whispered again, and grabbed the aerosol cans before she leaped out of the van. If she could deprive them of at least this much of the damaging chemical, maybe the rest of the captured shifters would have a fighting chance. She pressed herself against the outside of the van, hardly daring to breathe, and as soon as she felt the shocks depress with the weight of someone stepping into the back, she ran toward the truck.

She placed the cans in the truck bed, and watched in dismay as the van rolled forward, carrying the captives away from her. Away from potential rescue.

Billie scrambled into the truck's driver's side. They might see her following them, but what else could she do? She snapped her seatbelt on and took off with a lurch, keeping the headlights off. Just as she made it to Main Avenue, the van turned left onto another street. If she went straight, crossing Main Avenue, she could intersect them the next street over.

Billie had spent a day and a half captured by these people, these monsters who treated people... like animals. The phrase seemed particularly inappropriate. Neither humans nor animals should face the horrors the shifters had had to endure. But Stan and the others had been trapped by them for much longer, and she wasn't going to let them just drive away.

Billie turned the truck down the next street, guessing at where the van was. She sped up. She wasn't going to chase them. She was going to stop them in their tracks. The truck burst out of the narrow side street just as the van pulled into view. The vehicles collided with a crunch and shatter of glass, the truck t-boning the van right behind the driver's door. Billie slammed on the brakes, but the momentum still carried them across the intersection. The van tipped and clattered onto its side, two wheels spinning in the air.

Billie took a second to assure that she was, in fact, still alive. Pretty much unharmed, too. She didn't even feel the urge to shift. This adrenaline coursing through her came from determination, not fear. She yanked the seat belt off and grabbed a pocket knife from the truck's console. The truck's front bumper was dented inward and the headlights shattered, but the old truck was hardly even damaged. The van, though, was a mess. Its back door hung partially open. Billie yanked it the rest of the way.

A large owl flapped out as soon as there was enough space for it to fly through. Billie used the pocket knife to cut the zip ties off the other two. Stan was bleeding. The teen boy next to him was unconscious. As soon as Billie freed the boy, Stan scooped him up and took off as well.

"Wait!" Billie yelled after them, but none of them did. She heard some scrabbling from the front of the van, beyond the partition wall. No way was she sticking around long enough to wrangle with the kidnappers again.

The truck was still driveable. Stan sprinted down the street. Billie started the truck and headed in the same direction. Stan glanced over his shoulder at the truck, the streetlights flashing in his eyes, and then darted to the side, disappearing into someone's yard.

They think I'm chasing them, Billie realized. Well, she *was*, but not to try to capture them again. A few blocks away from downtown, she parked the truck, pulled her clothes free, and shifted. Bobcat paws landed on the asphalt. She lifted her nose to the sky, sorting through the many scents. The owl flapped by overhead, trailing after it the scent of Scarlet and fear. Billie raced in the same direction it flew.

Billie couldn't see them most of the time, but she managed to keep the scent trail of the shifters all the way out of the city and deep into the forest. A little thrill went through her when the trail led right to the mouth of a small cave. *She* had a cave, a safe space stocked with food and extra clothes, back in Juniper. It wasn't anything her mother had ever told her to have, nothing they'd set up together. The cave had been her idea, a hidden place she could go to in either animal or human form. Seeing that these shifters also had a cave felt like validation of her own instincts. A strange, small victory.

Inside the cave, the owl unfolded to human form, becoming a beautiful but weathered woman with silver-streaked dark hair that nearly reached her waist. She knelt and lit a camping lamp. Stan moved a slab of rock aside with an echoing scrape, revealing a large trunk with a creaking lid. Billie unfolded to human. The woman handed her a blanket from inside the trunk, but just as Billie wrapped it around her shoulders, Stan said, "I'm going to ask this one more time. Who the hell are you?"

Billie looked up into the face of the tall, burly man. Her dull human eyes were still adapting to the dim light. Even in human form, he had a menacing bear-like presence about him.

Before Billie could open her mouth to explain who she was, Travis and Samantha emerged from the shadows. They were both dressed but barefoot, wearing clothes that clearly didn't fit them. Billie nearly melted with the relief of knowing they'd been hiding out here and not captured. The owl woman rushed to them first, scooping them into a hug. Stan followed. The boy he'd been carrying was just starting to wake up, lifting a hand to his head with a wince.

Billie stepped back, tears biting at her eyes as she watched this family reunion. Which she was definitely not a part of. There was such an intimate ease to the way they embraced, tousled each other's hair, patted each other on the back. Billie pulled the blanket a little tighter around herself.

Travis's eyes met hers and he motioned for her to come closer. She hesitated, but he waved more insistently, and Billie tentatively stepped closer to the group, all eyes returning to her.

"I'm Billie Blackwater," she told them. "My dad says he's your friend. He brought me down here to meet all of you. I haven't... known any other shifters since my mom died."

The owl woman stepped forward, holding her blanket up with one hand, and wrapped the other arm around Billie in a hug. Billie tensed, but the touch didn't feel like a shock or an invasion the way a stranger's touch normally did. This hug filled her with a warm glow. Like Travis had. The way—she realized as sense memory flooded back in—the way her mother's touch had. Billie softened and leaned into the hug, overwhelmed by such a strange mix of joy and grief and hope and sorrow.

Her name was Helen, Billie remembered from her dad's cursory overview of the family. She was the woman in the white go-go boots, the mother of Travis and all his siblings. After a moment, Helen stepped back and Billie found herself wishing the hug had lasted longer. Helen looked around at the others and then said, "Jeffrey?" Travis's older brother: the first one who had disappeared. All of them shook their heads to indicate they hadn't seen him, and even Billie could feel the weight of his absence, this missing man she'd never met, and now probably never would.

"I'm going to go take a look around," Caleb said as he pulled his boots on. He'd spent the night in Chloe and Luke's spare bedroom, waking up every few minutes panicking at the unfamiliar creaks of the house or the horrific images remembered from the previous day. He used to be the type who could sleep anywhere, but he'd apparently gotten so comfortable in Billie's cabin that anywhere else put him on edge. Plus the horror show that he knew was outside, of course.

"You can't go," Chloe pleaded. "It's too dangerous!"

"It won't hurt just to take a drive."

Chloe chewed her lip. "You'll come back, right?"

Caleb hesitated. He liked being there with Chloe. With Luke, not so much, but the guy spent most of the day doing some dull spreadsheet work on his computer, and was otherwise usually absorbed in TV or video games, and never questioned why he and Chloe were talking about rocks all the time. Still, he didn't want to overstay his welcome, make things more awkward than they already were.

"If you want me to," he said.

"Yes!" Chloe nearly shrieked.

"Just a quick drive," he said. "Don't you want to know what's going on out there?"

"Not in detail, no," she said.

"Fair," Caleb said. "Broad picture only."

Caleb opened the kitchen door, but he took only one step outside before he spotted the mountain lion crouched only a few feet away. He stopped in his tracks, watching the animal watch him. For a disorienting moment, he thought it might have been Billie. It wasn't her preferred form, but he'd watched her shift into a mountain lion back at the abandoned timber mill where the Scarlet Monster had taken him. There was something almost human about the way the mountain lion looked at him. Had Billie come home and jealously stalked him here?

But no, this mountain lion had the same signs of Scarlet poisoning that the other animals in town did: bulked up muscles, missing fur and patches of raw skin, aggressive and deranged demeanor. Caleb's hand was still on the doorknob. He let it slip off, and took a hesitant step toward the car, keeping his eyes on the mountain lion. He hadn't taken Scarlet, didn't have a vial on him like when he'd been attacked before. Yet the mountain lion lifted its nose to the air to sniff, and before he could take a second step, it pounced. Caleb backpedaled and yanked the door open, slamming it behind him just in time. The mountain lion let out a bizarre-sounding growl.

"What was that?" Chloe dropped a plate and it shattered on the kitchen floor.

Something slammed against the outside of the door once more, but not again. Luke shouted from the other room to ask if everything was okay, but didn't come in to check. Caleb pulled the blinds on the kitchen door down. Chloe bent the blinds with one finger to peer out. The mountain lion jumped onto Caleb's car, curling up on the hood like an oversized housecat.

"Wow," she said. "Guess you're not going anywhere after all!"

Caleb frowned. "It shouldn't have attacked me, though."

Chloe let the blinds snap back to shape and knelt down to clean up the pieces of the broken plate. She shoved the pieces into the trash below the sink. Then she just sat there, staring at the pipes below the sink until Caleb asked her what was wrong.

"What if it's in the water now?" she said, pointing at the pipes. "All the water. We've been drinking it, cooking with it."

Caleb considered that the euphoria he'd felt after eating dinner last night might not have been solely the result of Chloe's cooking and company. He looked at his own arms, hands, searching for the tell-tale signs of sunburn-like redness and peeling that the other Scarlet addicts always had. So far, nothing, but would it creep up on him over time? Would he become a monster before he even knew it?

"If it's in the water, that's going to complicate things," he said. He offered a hand to help Chloe stand, but she ignored it, staying on the floor.

"It should be diluted, though," Chloe said. "It must affect animals worse than it does humans, for some reason, but it can't possibly be concentrated enough…"

"Mouse did dump quite a lot in the river."

"Even so."

Caleb shrugged. "Maybe it's enough that the animals can smell it on us. If they're getting desperate enough, that might be all it takes. I'm pretty sure that's what happened to my dad. Remember? He said he'd been swimming just before he got attacked."

A growl came from outside, and the sound of the car's shocks creaking as the mountain lion jumped off of it. Caleb swallowed the thick lump that tightened his throat.

"Plus," Caleb said, remembering the moose and the owl in front of the cabin, "they're all eating each other. That's got to compound everything."

That also probably meant that by the time this all met its peak, it would be only the biggest, most dangerous animals that were left. He chose not to voice this implication, but from Chloe's worried expression, he guessed she'd reached a similar conclusion.

Caleb pulled out his phone. There was no news being reported about what was happening to Juniper, no indications that it was happening anywhere else. He found a few social media posts from tourists who had been run out of town, but the pictures and videos were Bigfoot-blurry and had consistent explanations.

He texted Brock, "You staying safe?" and a few minutes later, Brock sent back, "Dude, Reverend got attacked by a goose!" Caleb checked in with a few other people around town and got stories of other people being attacked or going missing as well—people he knew wouldn't have been taking Scarlet. Apparently, a lot of people in town had essentially moved into the church, where they were having a prayer-a-thon or something to try to rid the town of demons.

Those who had been out told him that all of the shops on Miners Avenue had closed up, and Mitch had marked all the rooms at the Silver Coin as booked, even though there was hardly anyone in the hotel. One thing was for sure: Juniper was dying. No one from outside seemed to know about it, or care. They'd end up as a short chapter in some Haunted Colorado book, the mountain community that became a ghost town nearly overnight.

Chloe was probably right—the Scarlet was in the water, marking everyone in town as a potential target for the animals.

"Sure you don't know any water purification spells?"

She blinked at him, uncomprehending for a moment. He offered his hand again and this time she took it, hauling herself up to her feet.

"Um," she said. "We can keep looking through those books I have."

"Let's do that," Caleb said. Because what else could they do but hide from the horrors of the world? At least they could hide together.

A storm had rumbled in during the early hours of the morning, blowing a chill wind through the mouth of the cave. Beads of dampness dripped down the walls. Billie leaned against Travis, her head resting on his shoulder, letting that small contact between them fill her with a warm sensation that almost covered up all the terribleness of the last few days. Almost.

"What do we do now?" Travis asked. He had one arm around Samantha, absently stroking his sister's hair. "Sam and I have been hiding out here for two days. We already ate most of the food that was stashed."

"What the racoons hadn't eaten," Samantha mumbled. The girl still looked like she was asleep. They'd all taken turns pretending to sleep, but Billie was pretty sure none of them had gotten much rest.

"Did you call Uncle Virgil?" Stan asked.

"The number was disconnected," Travis said.

Stan grumbled, a sound that was almost bear-like even in his human form.

"Your mother's family," Helen said to Billie. She'd told Billie she could call her "mom" if she wanted, since everyone did. Billie chose to keep calling her Helen. "Do you know how to contact any of them?"

Billie shook her head. "Her name was Valerie. Dad says her last name was Smith, but I suspect that was a fake. I think she was running from something. Maybe... maybe something like what happened to us. I don't know. She never told me anything."

Alex, Travis's teen brother, picked up small rocks from the cave floor and threw them at the wall, creating a pattern of echoing clicks. They'd made him a makeshift sling, but he likely had a broken arm and a concussion from the van crash. He hadn't said much in the hours they'd been in the cave. Billie wondered if he blamed her for his injuries. She kept going over the scene again and again, wondering if there had been another way to break them free that wouldn't have hurt him.

After a long, sad moment, Billie said, "There was supposed to be a raid. Kaitlyn was using our blood to make Scarlet. The DEA are supposed to raid the storage rooms soon; I assume someone got tipped off and that's why they were trying to move all of you."

"To make what?" Alex asked.

"Scarlet," Billie said. "It's a drug. At high doses it makes people transform. Not quite like we do, but into a sort of demon-like creature."

"Did they…" Alex stopped throwing rocks and dug his fingers into the dirt of the cave floor. "The ones in the van, did they die?"

Billie shook her head. "I didn't stick around to find out."

"I hope they died," he muttered.

"*Alex*," Helen said.

"*What?*" he said, defiant. His mother frowned at him, but said nothing.

Billie stared at the cave's floor. She thought of Mitch asking her to kill Toby, and the sickened feeling she had gotten when she considered doing it, the way she'd vehemently declared, and believed, that she was not a murderer. If it turned out she had killed the men in the van, though, the ones who had captured and abused her and all the people hiding here in the cave, she wasn't sure she would feel much remorse.

"If there was a raid," Helen said, "then they all should have been caught, and we can go back home once it's safe."

"But how will we ever *know* it's safe?" Travis said. "What if they're still out there?"

"It's never entirely safe," Stan said. "But we can't hide forever."

"I'll go," Billie said. "If I can get back to your house, my phone is there. I can contact my dad. He'll know what happened, and what to do. If it comes down to it, we can get all of you out of town. You can come up to Juniper with us."

Not that Juniper was necessarily safer, not if Elliot Moran was part of the Scarlet operations. But it was all she had to offer.

"I'll go with you to the house," Travis said.

Billie started to protest, but she didn't know the way, and wouldn't want to go alone even if she did.

"When the rain stops," Helen said.

"When the rain stops," Billie agreed.

Until then, she had a *lot* of questions she was dying to ask, and this was the first chance she'd had to ask any of them.

SATURDAY

Caleb and Chloe had spent most of the last two days going through her collection of stones and looking over the various books on her shelf, many of which had been liberally scribbled in, whole passages crossed out, notes fit into the margins in her neat and nearly microscopic handwriting.

The vibrations of all the stones spread out across the floor filled the room. Caleb flopped backward against the foot of the bed, his head pounding. "I think I need a break." He reached for the onyx and pressed it to his forehead. The noise quieted. "Are you sure you can't just switch this off?"

"Are you sure you would even want that?" Chloe asked.

Caleb didn't really have an answer. It was all still strange and new, and he wasn't sure how this new facet of himself was going to fit into his life once everything returned to normal. If it ever returned to normal.

Luke tapped on the doorframe then and announced, "I'm going to pick up some more beer, you need anything?"

"All of the stores are closed, honey," Chloe said.

"Still?"

"Yes, baby," Chloe said. "The animals are still crazy, it's too dangerous to go outside."

"Oh," Luke said. He went back out into the living room, closing the door behind him.

Exasperated, Caleb finally spat out, "Why are you with that… that dolt?!?"

"Excuse me," Chloe said, but her eyes were sparkling, her lips in a grin. "*Dolt*?"

"He's mundane and mediocre in every way. You're extraordinary. You should be with someone who's more… more like…"

"More like you?"

Caleb paused. "I was going to say more like *you*, but, yeah, here we are." And he *was* like her. They had the same magic. They saw the world in the same way. She was more like him than anyone he'd ever known.

Chloe kept smiling. "Caleb, I love Luke *because* he's mundane. Because he's a bit boring. He keeps me grounded. The world is so often trying to sweep me away in a chaotic whirlwind. Luke is my tether. I'd be so lost without him."

Caleb dropped his gaze to the floor. A muscle twitched in his jaw and he tried to keep from grinding his teeth. When Chloe ran her fingertips along his arm, it sent an almost electric shock of desire through him. He looked at her, brows bunched in confusion at the unexpectedly tender touch.

"We have an open marriage, though. An agreement that we can pursue other partners if we really want to. So, you and I could have an affair." Chloe ran her fingers lightly up his arm again. She looked him in the eyes, a mischievous curl to her lips. "I think I'd like that."

Caleb had *not* been expecting that. His hands twitched with the urge to draw her in closer. As if sensing that he wanted to reach for her, she scooted back, just out of reach.

"*But*," she said, "it's the secrecy, the jealousy, that makes situations like this so full of conflict. That's what I don't want. Transparency— for everyone involved—is the only way this works."

Everyone involved. "You mean Billie," Caleb said, and a weight of guilt descended on him as soon as he said her name.

"I *like* Billie," Chloe said. "I want to be friends with her. And I don't want anything to compromise that friendship. Do you think she would be okay with this? With us?"

Caleb thought about that. He remembered the way Billie would lift his hands back up to her skin if they slipped away, how needy she was with his touch, how she avoided even casual physical contact with anyone else. He had told her about the other girls he'd been with in Boulder, and she'd been so hurt by that confession. It had taken a long time for her to fully soften to him again. He recalled how close he had come to losing her then, and how much that had scared him.

Caleb shook his head and said softly, "No. No, I don't think she would."

Chloe returned his sad smile. "Well, then. She's too important to both of us. So nothing can happen between us."

Caleb shoved his hands into his pockets. He was being stupid, letting his hormones lead him instead of his heart. This wasn't college anymore; he wasn't going to let himself make the same mistakes again. He'd changed. Though apparently not as much as he wanted to believe, since he'd indulged this crush as deeply as he had.

"I miss her," he whispered.

And all of a sudden, it all flooded in. He *did* miss Billie, a lot. He'd been mad at her when she left, and none of those things that had bothered him so much seemed to mean anything anymore. He just wanted her back. Their fight before she left had simply been that same old fear of losing her bubbling up again, and him being a jerk about it instead of just telling her how he felt.

Chloe tapped a finger on her lips. "I know you do. We can be friends, though, without it turning into anything more. Right?"

Friend-zoned, Caleb thought, but the term seemed childish. He *did* want to be friends with Chloe, and he wanted to keep learning about this magic that she'd awoken in him. He'd be happy to have Chloe as his mentor, and his friend. "Right," he agreed, and meant it.

Her phone dinged then, and she picked it up, frowning at what she read. "Huh."

"What is it?"

She blinked up at him. "Oh. That clothing shop I had a weird feeling about?"

"I remember," Caleb prompted. "At the Silver Coin, after we went to see my dad."

"It was apparently sitting on top of a major Scarlet lab."

She turned the phone toward him and he took it and thumbed through the article. "Wait, this was in Durango?" He skimmed for any mentions of people involved. Knowing Billie, she'd have found herself wrapped up in this somehow. No one was named, it just said that the DEA had raided and uncovered equipment and product.

"Right in the middle of the town," Chloe said, wonderingly.

Caleb handed her the phone back, and picked up his own, sending a message to Billie: *Heard there was a Scarlet raid in Durango. Hope you're okay.* To Chloe, he said, "These… feelings, messages you get, is that part of the earth magic? Why would you be picking up on something like this, so far away?"

Chloe had been scrolling the article again. "Huh? Oh. I'm not sure. It's just something I've always done. You don't get them?"

Caleb shook his head. If he was receptive to psychic messages, they got lost in the noise of everything else going on in his brain.

"Maybe there's hope for us now, with the Scarlet," Chloe said, but she didn't look hopeful, not at all. She chewed on an already ragged nail, and she was staring off into space again, though not quite as distant as she had been when she'd gotten the message about the store.

"Okay," Caleb said. "So you were about to tell me about the precious metals."

Chloe snapped back to the moment and picked up the book again and opened it to the page on silver.

A coyote and a bobcat emerged from a cave in the forest south of Durango, eyes and ears and noses vigilant for any threats. It was dusk, the sky purple with the waning light, and silent aside from the drip of water still sliding off of the pine needles from the storm that had finally passed. In human form, Billie would have been chilled, but wrapped in her bobcat fur, the temperature was just about perfect. The coyote led the way and the bobcat followed, weaving through the forest.

They circled the house several times before venturing closer. The rain had washed away most human scents, replacing them with the petrichor of fresh wet soil. Gradually, their circles grew tighter, until the coyote stepped tentatively onto the back porch. The back door had been left partially open. Still in animal form, he nosed it wide. Billie kept watch outside while the coyote explored the house. After a long couple of minutes, Travis came back out, in human form now, dressed in black t-shirt and jeans.

"It's clear," he said.

Still a bobcat, Billie padded in the door after him. He tossed some clothes for her onto the couch. Billie glanced at them and hesitated.

Quirking up one side of his mouth, he said, "I've seen you before."

Billie hissed at him and he raised his hands and turned his back. She unfolded to human form and reached for the clothes.

Travis looked over his shoulder at her as she buttoned the flannel shirt. "Will you stay here with us?"

"I don't know." She sat down on the Lesniks' couch with a weary sigh.

She'd been so eager to meet these other shifters, and she would always treasure those conversations they'd had in the cave. Even though they didn't know her mother's family, they'd helped her understand where she'd come from and how she fit into the world. How there were shifters in all parts of the world, how those who had come to North America from elsewhere had to learn new animal forms that fit with the local ecosystems. They'd confirmed things she'd only guessed at, dispelled beliefs she'd always held, and she held each of their answers close to her heart like a secret locket.

And yet, she still felt like an outsider with them. These had been *their* stories, not hers. Parallel, perhaps, but not intersecting. She was a visitor here, an interloper intruding on their family intimacy. And Travis, well. She watched him as he continued to search and secure the house. He was attractive, for sure, but she didn't feel at home with him like she did with Caleb. She was pretty sure he was more interested in *what* she was than *who* she was.

She missed Caleb. She missed sleeping in her own bed, shifting in her own cave. She missed the familiarity of Juniper, knowing the paths so well she could practically run them with her eyes closed. She even missed Mitch, just a little bit, with his faux-gangster bravado. It was time to go home.

Her phone was still on the coffee table where she'd left it, but of course the battery was dead. She lifted it hopefully. "Have a cord that will charge this?"

Travis inspected the flip phone, and then said, "Good thing my mom never throws anything away."

He dug in a storage closet and came back with a box of cords. After a couple of tries, Billie found one that worked and plugged it in. Travis went back upstairs while she sat on the floor next to the outlet and sorted through missed calls and texts.

There were a lot from Caleb, most of them just attempts to check in, and also several from Robyn, about the sale of the cabin, which she'd blissfully forgotten about until now. The most recent one from Caleb said, *Heard there was a Scarlet raid in Durango. Hope you're okay.*

Billie leaned her head back against the wall and let out a sigh of relief. She sent back *!!!!!* and then ***Im safe***.

"They did the raid," Billie told Travis when he came back downstairs.

He held up his phone—the screen cracked so badly it was hard to read. "I found it too." He sat on the floor next to her and showed her an article saying a raid had uncovered Scarlet production operating out of the hidden underground rooms of downtown Durango. Three suspects had been arrested in connection.

"Kaitlyn's one of them, for sure." He pointed to a line mentioning a local chemistry professor that made a snarky comparison to Breaking Bad.

She'd be back someday, Billie realized, thinking about how her own father had returned to Juniper after being released from prison. Would Kaitlyn be repentant about what she'd done, or continue to feel like she was the real victim?

"The monster's still out there," Billie said. "It's just had its fangs removed."

Travis grinned at that. "We'll be better prepared next time it attacks."

"Hopefully there won't be a next time," Billie said, but she wasn't confident. There was always a next time, always a new threat. The brief history Stan and Helen had been able to share with Billie about the periodic witch hunts of various shifter populations around the world had assured her of that. Both Stan and Helen had told her stories of family members being forced out of their home, coming to the U.S. for supposed safety. The stories went back as many generations as they could count. They always needed to be ready to shift and run.

Billie called the saloon and got a hold of Lisa. She was actually relieved to hear the other woman's voice, and even more relieved when she told Billie her dad was there too.

"We were so worried," Lisa whispered. "When we found the truck without you in it, we feared the worst."

"I'm okay," Billie said. "Tell my dad I'm at their house. And I'm ready to go home."

She made eye contact with Travis as she said that last part, and something seemed to shut down in him, as if he'd finally resolved that nothing would happen between them. Lisa said something about trying to get off work early so they could come out there. "Yeah, okay." Billie hung up the phone and looked away with both relief and sadness coursing through her. Rather than deal with any of that, she said, "I'll go get the others. You keep watch here. If anyone comes, run and meet me partway."

"Sure you can find your way?" Travis asked.

"I can find it," Billie said.

She left her phone plugged in. On the back porch, she took off the clothes she'd just put on. Their own scent trails were still fresh and she followed them back to the cave.

Once all the Lesniks were home—or at least all the ones still living and not in jail—Billie sat on the front porch, getting out of their way so they could settle back in to their house. A truck rumbled into the driveway, and Billie actually smiled as she recognized that rusty, mud-splattered jalopy, with the crack in the back windshield and the broken side mirror. The front fender was twisted from where she'd crashed into the van, but they'd already replaced the broken headlights. Lisa waved enthusiastically at Billie from the passenger seat, and Billie gave a little groan but lifted a hand to wave back.

Then the front door burst open and Stan stomped out, a shotgun lifted and pointed right at the new arrivals. Billie's heartrate sped up, and she jumped to her feet, reaching toward Stan with words caught in her throat. He gave her a warning glance, and kept the gun pointed while Billie's dad stepped out of the truck, hands raised. Lisa hesitated, but then did the same.

"It's just us, Stan," her dad said. "Keith Blackwater. You remember me, yeah?"

"The witch and the murderer." There wasn't any venom in his tone, but Stan kept the gun aimed.

"It was manslaughter," her dad said, voice cool and calm. "An accident I regret every damn day of my life."

"Last time I saw you," Stan said, "you cheated me in a game of Seven Card Stud."

"Only because you'd already stacked the deck."

Stan lowered the gun and Billie's dad lowered his hands. Billie let out the breath she'd been holding and clattered down the steps toward her dad and Lisa.

"Baby doll, I'm so glad you're alright," he said. He opened his arms to invite an embrace, but let her choose whether to step into it or not. She did, just for a moment, and it wasn't so bad. More awkward than anything. Once she let go, Lisa threw her arms around her and squeezed, rocking side to side and squealing.

"Okay, way too much," Billie said as she extracted herself and stepped away. She looked between the two of them. "You're not mad I took the truck?"

"Furious," her dad said with a smile. "But you're safe, and I assume you had some role in getting everyone out before the raid, so that's more important."

Lisa gave Billie a knowing wink. Why had Stan called her a witch? She couldn't be a shifter too, but did she have some other abilities?

Stan clapped Billie's dad on the back and invited them all inside. Several of the Lesniks were already in the kitchen, cooking everything that wasn't expired.

Billie's phone vibrated and she looked at the message from Caleb: *Can we talk, please?* She hesitated. They definitely needed to talk, to repair what had almost broken between them. But this was the last evening she was going to get with the Lesniks. She needed to spend this time with them.

Soon, she sent back. And then, *I love u.*

It took a few minutes, but eventually he responded, *I love you too.*

Billie smiled in relief, and put her phone away for the night. In the morning, Billie and her dad would drive back to Juniper. Then Billie could tell Caleb all about her trip, and find out what she'd missed back home while she was gone.

SUNDAY

The drive home was, overall, less awkward than the drive to Durango had been. Still, Billie was ready to be out of the car by the time they were winding along the familiar twisty mountain roads outside of Juniper. It was a day later than she'd told Mitch she would be back, but surprisingly, he'd sent no angry or sarcastic messages about her absence like she'd expected.

It was right around the Silver Coin that Billie started to realize something was off. Boards had been crossed over the Silver Coin's entrance, with messy paint that read, "Stay Out." Billie craned her neck at it as they passed, confused. Something thumped underneath the truck's carriage. Billie turned forward in alarm.

"What was that?"

She couldn't quite read the expression on her dad's face, but he kept his tone even as he said, "I think I hit a squirrel or rabbit or something, that's all."

Billie frowned and said nothing as they climbed the last couple of switchbacks to get into town. They were the only car on the road, and had been for quite a while. They rounded the corner and Miners Avenue came into view. Shops were closed, and boards covered the windows of Mouse's dispensary. The place looked like a ghost town.

Billie's dad parked the truck in front of the cabin. The car wasn't there. Billie swallowed thickly, her throat tightening as she recalled Caleb telling her that he might not be there when she got back. But *no one* was anywhere in sight, which had her a little more concerned at the moment. What the hell had happened here while she was gone?

Just as Billie opened the truck door and reached for her bag, the moose stepped around the corner of the shops across the street. Or what used to be a moose. Its back legs were trunks of red muscle, and its front legs had elongated so much that it practically stood upright. The tips of its antlers were sharp, bifurcated points, and small red wings flared from its back. Billie paused, hand hovering over her bag, gawking at the creature. The moose noticed her as well. It lifted its head and sniffed at the air, its eyes growing wide. Then it charged.

Billie stared dumbfounded for another moment, and then dove back into the truck. Her dad followed, shouting a string of curses, and they shut the doors just as the moose slammed into the side of the truck. The moose backed up and rammed again. The truck rocked so hard the wheels briefly left the ground. A crack splintered across the windshield. Her dad tried to start the engine, but the force of the impact shook the keys out of his hands. He scrambled to find them on the floorboards.

Billie fumbled for her phone and called Caleb. "Pick up, pick up!" she pleaded.

"Well, look who finally decided to call back," Caleb said, snark thick in his voice.

The moose circled the truck, and some kind of bird landed on the hood, pecking aggressively at the windshield. Ratty feathers made it look like it was halfway through a bad molt. Its eyes practically glowed red.

"What the hell happened to Juniper?" she shouted. "There's a… a wendigo or something attacking the truck."

"A what? Wait, are you back?"

"Yes! I'm at the cabin, where the hell are you? It looks like someone's been feeding Scarlet to the animals."

"Hold on, I'm coming to get you."

"*Hold on?*" The moose kept prowling in a circle around the truck and the bird flapped and slammed its body against the windshield. But Caleb had already hung up.

If she shifted, could she outrun the moose? She wasn't sure. And where could she go? This thing had wings, and it could track her scent. At best, maybe she could get out to Juniper Ridge and hide in a cave or nook that was too small for this monster to get into. But—she glanced at the bird, still hurling itself against the windshield—there was clearly more than one monster around.

"They're after me," she told her dad. "My blood. You should get out while you can. Run."

"I'm not leaving you."

Suddenly she noticed something clanging around in the truck bed. She looked back and saw the two aerosol cans rolling against their still-secured luggage. The spray that kept her from shifting.

"I have an idea." Billie shoved the tiny back window open as far as it would go and stuck her head and arms out.

"What the hell are you doing?" Her dad grabbed at her legs, but she kicked him away. The metal of the window's track dug into her stomach as she leaned out, grabbing for the closest can. She got hold of it in the same second the moose lunged at her. She sprayed right in its face, and the creature fell back, writhing in pain. Billie crawled all the way out of the window and got to her feet, standing in the truck bed. The bird dove at her, taking a chunk of flesh out of her arm. She sprayed and the bird fell away with a high-pitched shriek.

Billie clutched at her arm. The pain started small, but was gradually growing into a sharp sting. And it was bleeding. A lot. She pulled up the hem of her shirt to wrap over the wound. Her vision was beginning to blur, and that lightheadedness she'd experienced in the underground room came back in full force. Still clutching the spray can, she edged over to look at the moose. It was making awful sounds: gurgling, screaming grunts. The elongated front legs were shrinking before her eyes. Billie's arm hurt like hell, but it was nothing compared to the pain she remembered when she'd been sprayed while half shifted. The moose kept transforming, wings retracting into its back. Finally, it lay there, a bloody mess, missing patches of its fur, its tongue hanging out and panting, looking exactly like a moose that had been hit by a car.

Billie's dad got out of the truck as another vehicle pulled up.

"Billie!" Caleb's voice rang through the air. Her head swam, and her vision was graying out like the static on an old TV. His familiar voice was a welcome beacon, an she moved blindly toward it.

The pain was getting worse in her arm, and she nearly doubled over. Her shins hit the tailgate and she lost balance. Caleb caught her, easily scooping her into his arms.

"Caleb, there's more of them coming," said a woman's voice.

"Shit," Caleb said. Billie lifted the can to try to tell him about the spray, but found it hard to form any words. He got her inside and laid her on the couch.

"She's hurt," Billie's dad said.

"I can see that," Caleb snapped. "Chloe, can you…"

"You can do it," the woman's voice said. "Just like I showed you."

Billie held the spray can out again, but it slipped from her fingers, falling to the coffee table and then rolling to the floor with a loud clang. "Stops… the transformation," she finally got out. But then Caleb laid his palm over her arm, just above the wound.

Billie opened her eyes with sudden clarity. The pain was fading away, and she could breathe again, could see without looking through a fog. The immediacy of the injury lessened by the second.

"What the hell?" She tried to sit up.

"Shh, shh," the woman said, gently pressing her back down. Billie recognized her now: Chloe, the tourist who had been at a real estate showing at the Shadow Ridge house when Billie first saw her mother's ghost make the rocking chair move. Caleb kept one hand clasped over Billie's bloody arm, his eyes closed and forehead bunched. He was so beautiful with his hair dangling into his eyes and a light sheen of sweat on his skin. Billie relaxed, letting the pain rush out of her. After a moment, Caleb let go and sat back with a dazed expression. He dropped something on the floor with a thunk, and Chloe handed him a shiny black stone. Caleb grabbed for it and let out a relieved moan.

Billie's dad handed her some paper towels, and Billie took them, wiping the blood from her arm. It still ached a little, but the wound was closed, looking like the scab of several days' healing rather than a fresh injury. She wadded up the bloody towels and set them on the coffee table.

Caleb started to put the black stone in his pocket, but Chloe said, "We have to cleanse it," and he handed it over to her.

"*What*," Billie said, "just happened?"

Caleb was sitting on the floor, and he looked up at her, their eyes locking for the first time since this drama started. There was something so intense in his gaze that for a moment, all questions, all words, fled her mind. Then, he got to his feet, sat on the couch next to her, and... wow... It had been a while since he'd kissed her quite like *that*.

Billie's dad cleared his throat, but Caleb didn't stop. After another moment, he pulled away, and Billie wished he hadn't. He touched her face lightly with his fingertips. "Are you okay?"

Billie caught her breath, feeling heat rush through her cheeks. "Yeah," she whispered.

"There are more monsters," Chloe said. "They're surrounding the house."

Billie blinked at her, having forgotten she was there. "They're after me."

"Why?" Caleb asked, his expression darkening slightly.

"Scarlet is made from shifter blood," Billie said.

"*Shifter* blood?" Chloe repeated, and Billie realized she'd just outed herself to this near stranger. What was she doing here anyway? "Oh, I *knew* there was something special about you!"

Billie reluctantly extracted herself from Caleb's comfortable embrace. She found the spray can underneath the coffee table. She picked it up and held it out. "This worked against them. It inhibits shifting, and it seems to reverse the Scarlet transformation."

Chloe reached for the can, and the second she touched it, she said, "Oh! It's silver. I'm sure there's other stuff in it, but it's primarily silver. Colloidal silver. Makes perfect sense, actually."

Nothing about this made perfect sense to Billie. Chloe hadn't smelled or tasted the spray or anything. It was unmarked, nothing but a generic aluminum can. Chloe handed the bottle to Caleb.

"Okay, yeah," he said, nodding. "I can feel it. Silver, like with werewolves."

All the tenderness she'd felt toward Caleb after that kiss faded in a flash of anger. "I'm *not* a—"

"No, I know," he said, raising his hands defensively. "But if there's something about silver that interferes with shifting, that's probably where the stories came from. The silver bullet thing." Billie still glared at him. He lifted the can. "Do you have any more of this?"

"There's one more in the truck."

But then her dad held up the other can, shaking it. "Sorry, baby doll. I've got it, but it's nearly empty."

"Enchanted Mountain," Caleb said suddenly. "There's colloidal silver in there. I saw bottles of it."

"Good, let's go," Billie's dad said. Caleb set the can on the table and stood.

"You can't go out there," Chloe said.

"Why?"

She tugged at Caleb's shirt, and there was something intimate in the gesture that made Billie narrow her eyes suspiciously at the two of them.

"Oh." Caleb looked down sheepishly at the shirt, splattered with

Billie's blood.

"I'll go," Chloe said. "I haven't used local water in more than a day, so I shouldn't be a target."

"I'll go with you," Billie's dad said.

"Great!" Chloe chirped. Then, "Sorry, who are you?"

"I'm Keith. Billie's dad."

"And you're not…"

"A shapeshifter? No, I'm just a plain old human. And I've got a crowbar."

"Perfect!" Chloe nearly shouted, and the two of them were out the door before either Caleb or Billie could say anything. The door shut behind them, leaving Billie and Caleb alone together in the cabin.

Billie rose shakily to her feet, still lightheaded from the blood she'd lost. She and Caleb looked at each other for a long moment. All the anger and hardness he'd been holding when she left was gone, but there was something a little bit different about him, something she couldn't quite put her finger on.

"Your leg's better." That wasn't the only thing, but it was the most tangible one. He'd carried her without buckling or limping, and he stood up without wincing like he had ever since the Scarlet Monster attacked his leg.

He looked down at his leg as though he'd forgotten it existed. "Uh, yeah." He laughed.

"I'm sorry I didn't respond to your calls or texts," she said.

She opened her mouth to explain further, but before she could, he was kissing her again, and all the rest of her pain and fear melted away. When the kiss ended, he wrapped her into a tight hug.

"I was being an ass to you before you left."

"You were," she agreed.

"I know you have your own life," he said. "I just want to be part of it. Yeah?"

"Yeah." Tears bit at the backs of her eyes. "So, we're okay?"

He squeezed her a little tighter and nodded against her shoulder.

"We're okay."

Billie kept her hands on his arms as she pulled back and looked him in the eyes again. "So," she breathed. "What the hell happened here while I was gone?"

MONDAY

Chloe and Luke showed up at the cabin on Monday morning carrying a plastic tub full of squirt guns, jugs of water, and a few more bottles of silver to supplement the ones they'd stolen from Enchanted Mountain. The night before, Caleb had discovered a family of mice chewing their way through the cabin floorboards, crazed on Scarlet like all the other animals. After testing the colloidal silver on the mice, they'd confirmed that it had a similar effect to that spray Billie had brought back from Durango. So Chloe and Luke had left town on a supply run to track down more. They'd found they could dilute the silver pretty well with non-Scarlet poisoned water and it would still be effective.

"Hey, come look at this!" Chloe said as they set the tub inside the cabin door.

All night, the moose that had attacked Keith's truck had lain in the street where it had fallen after Billie sprayed it, panting like dying roadkill. Now, it was struggling to get to its feet.

Caleb looked over at Billie, who was fiddling with the particulate filtration mask Chloe and Luke had picked up for her. He motioned for her to come see, and moved so she had space to look out the window. She stood in front of him and he rubbed his hands affectionately over her upper arms.

"It's alive," she whispered.

It looked like hell, but it was, in fact, alive. More importantly, it looked like a moose again—no wings, no red eyes, so steroidal bulk. The moose shook its massive head and sauntered down the road on unsteady legs.

"Can it get re-infected if it drinks from the lake?" Chloe asked.

"Don't know," Billie said. "Guess we'll find out."

They'd considered just dumping the silver into the lake to counteract the Scarlet, but an internet search had told them that was unequivocally a bad idea—while colloidal silver was touted as having "healing properties," it could actually be pretty dangerous, even to people who weren't shifters. They'd opted for a more direct application instead. So all of them got to work mixing the silver and water, and filling the squirt guns. Even Luke helped out, asking surprisingly few dumb questions along the way. Billie wore her mask and thick garden gloves, and Caleb could tell she was trying to touch and breathe as little of the silver as she could.

After a while, a truck pulled up in front of the cabin. Joaquin stepped out of the driver's side and four other locals rode in the bed. Luke and Keith picked up the tub full of squirt guns, and Chloe held the door open for them. Billie adjusted her face mask. She zipped up a purple rain jacket and followed Caleb outside.

"Ready?" Caleb said to Joaquin.

Joaquin pulled his gun out of the back of the truck. "Let's do this," he said. "I'm sick of hiding in the church acting like some miracle's gonna save us."

"One catch," Caleb told him. "We're using these."

He held out a super soaker. Joaquin glanced back and forth between the toy and Caleb. He laughed.

"What the fuck is this?"

"I'm serious."

As if on cue, a stray cat bounded toward them, all the signs of

Scarlet transformation apparent in its red eyes and loose fur. Caleb turned the super soaker on it and the cat leaped into the air, doing a twisted flip to escape the spray, but instead of running away, it landed in a heap and started to transform back into a regular cat.

Joaquin stared wide-eyed at the mewling creature. Caleb shoved the super soaker into Joaquin's chest.

"Seriously. No real guns. This is what works."

Joaquin nodded in reverent awe at the writhing cat. Chloe and Keith passed out squirt guns and backup bottles of the silver solution to everyone Joaquin had brought, and that hunting group took off, presumably toward a trailhead that would take them into the forest.

Caleb gestured for the others to follow, and they carried the tub two blocks, encountering and neutralizing a couple of animals along the way.

"See, honey," Chloe said to Luke, "all that video game time is finally coming in handy."

At the church, they set the tub on the front steps and the others posted guard while Caleb banged on the door with a fist. He could hear movement inside, but no one answered until he shouted, "Reverend Provine! We need your help."

A few moments later, the door opened a crack, and the reverend peered out. His hair was a mess, and his face looked haggard, with dark circles under his eyes and dry, chapped lips. Past him in the dark interior of the church, Caleb estimated half of Juniper's population was camped out in the sanctuary.

"Mr. Mulligan." Reverend Provine opened the door wider. "Come in, please."

Caleb grabbed the handle of the tub and dragged it in after him. The others stayed outside. "You were right about the uselessness of 'earthly weapons.' Ready to fight some demons?" He tossed a small squirt gun. The reverend, who had been attempting to lock the door again, fumbled to catch it, then looked bewildered at the toy.

Caleb opened the tub and pulled out a squirming sack. He

dumped one of the transformed mice on the floor of the church. The crowd that had gathered around him gasped and backed up. The mouse stood on hind legs and hissed at them. It was nearly fully transformed: red wings flared out of its back, tiny claws elongated into talons, snout engorged and almost wolf-like.

Caleb slung the super soaker from his back and aimed it at the mouse. As soon as the water hit it, the creature shrieked and the wings began to shrink. He turned to the reverend, watching him watch all of this in astonishment. He held up the squirt gun Caleb had thrown at him, pinched between two fingers.

"Holy water?"

Caleb shook his head. "No, it's silver. Like for werewolves. You try plain old holy water on these things, you're going to get eaten." He gestured at the tub and turned toward the Juniper locals who had taken refuge in the church. "This is what we've got. It works. You going to help us reclaim the town or not?"

The crowd surged forward to claim the water guns. Caleb opened the church door. Chloe looked over her shoulder at him, her water gun aimed toward the street, ready should anything appear. She'd been afraid that going to the church would backfire on them, but Caleb had insisted it would work. Caleb gave her a wink as the people swarmed out after him and she grinned.

He reached for Billie and pulled her into a quick reassuring hug. He knew she was scared to go out there, but he was proud of her for doing it anyway. And he was so damn glad to have her back. She repositioned her facemask, and then all of them spread out through the town, looking for afflicted animals to de-transform.

WEDNESDAY

Nothing was normal, exactly, but people were starting to come out of hiding, and Billie thought that seemed like a step in the right direction. The animals they sprayed with the silver solution didn't transform again, even if they drank from the lake water. Many of them recovered, though some were too far gone.

The quarry was re-opening, and Caleb's alarm went off as the sky began to lighten. Billie reached for him, catching his arm and pulling him back into bed.

"Don't go," she whispered. She pulled him close, pressing as much of his skin against hers as she could. She'd thought before that Caleb was typical and mundane, but she knew now that wasn't true. He had a magical gift, a sixth sense for the vibrations of stones that she couldn't fully understand. *And* he could take pain away. He'd always been able to do that, somewhat, which must have been part of why she'd always craved his touch so much.

He kissed her but slid out of bed. "You'll be here when I get back?"

Billie propped herself up on her elbow and considered him. It was the same question she'd asked him before she left for the trip to Durango, but he asked it now in an entirely different tone. He'd done that before, taking things they'd said in anger and transforming them into something that brought them closer together. But what answer did he want?

She shrugged. "Maybe."

He looked over his shoulder at her, jeans pulled up but not buttoned yet. "Maybe? What do I have to do to convince you?"

But before she could come up with any clever reply, he'd leaped onto the bed again, and she tugged those jeans right back off of him.

Several hours after Caleb left for the quarry, Billie got a text from Mitch: *You still work here, or what?*

Billie considered the text for a few moments before she sent back: *You still hiding from squirrels, or what?*

Get your ass here in half an hour or you're fired.

1 hour, she sent back.

There was a long pause before he finally sent: *Fine.*

Billie grinned. Small victories. Maybe the start of some boundaries that could make working for Mitch a little more tolerable.

The phone buzzed again. She groaned. Mitch wasn't going to let her have this small win, was he? But when she flipped the phone open to look at the text, it was from Robyn. Billie closed the phone, not even reading the message. Robyn had called and texted several times while Billie was in Durango, and Caleb mentioned that she'd even stopped by. Billie looked around at the small cabin, suddenly not wanting to give it up. Maybe the developers Robyn had been courting wouldn't be interested anymore after the town had been overrun by zombie animals? One could only hope.

Caleb had taken the car to the quarry, so Billie stuck a loaded water gun into her back pocket and decided she'd hike over to the Silver Coin. On the way, she saw Heather and Chloe talking outside of Enchanted Mountain. The front window was still boarded up. Chloe had been the one who broke that window to get to the bottles of colloidal silver inside, but they appeared to be chatting amicably. From across the street, Billie waved to both of them and they waved back.

Mitch had taken the "Stay Out" sign off and opened the gate. Billie passed through the parking garage to go inside. One of the only vehicles in there was a dilapidated, mud-splattered truck that she recognized quite well. She touched the scratched hood. The truck hadn't been in good shape when they'd started the trip to Durango, but now it was a total wreck. There were still flecks of white paint on the bent front fender from ramming into the kidnappers' van.

What was her dad doing here? But then Billie remembered a conversation from a couple of weeks ago, which felt like lifetimes past. Mitch had offered him a job. Her throat clenched a bit, but less so than when she'd first been told. It would be okay. The two of them weren't totally good, maybe never would be, but things between them were a little better. When she saw him around the hotel, maybe she wouldn't immediately think of her mother falling to the ground in the backyard. Maybe she'd think instead of driving home from Durango, of dinner together with the Lesniks.

Nearly as soon as she was inside, Kim was shoving linens toward her and asking her to take them to a room on the fourth floor. Billie usually worked at the bar, but no one running around the Silver Coin at the moment seemed to be doing their regular job. Except for Mitch, who sat in one of the lobby chairs with his arm in a sling, yelling at everyone to work harder. Her dad stood on a ladder, fixing some wiring on the antler chandelier. Billie wrapped her arms around the bunch of linens and approached Mitch.

"Oh, look who it is," Mitch said. "You finally find yourself, kitty cat? You make peace with your screwed up inner child and learn how to love yourself and all that bullshit?"

"If I had," Billie said, "why would I be back here?"

"Because you love me." Mitch gave a cheesy grin.

"I got bills to pay, is all."

Mitch slapped his uninjured arm to his chest in mock heartache. Then he waved dismissively. "Good, then go, work. This clusterfuck has cost me way too much already. The sooner we open, the better."

Billie started to turn away, but then gestured at his injured arm. "I'm glad it wasn't worse."

They both knew exactly how bad it could have been. Suddenly there was no sarcasm in Mitch's response. "Yeah. Me, too. Thanks, kitty cat."

Her dad climbed down from the ladder. "Need me to do anything, baby doll?"

Billie rolled her eyes. "I need *both* of you to stop calling me silly diminutive nicknames."

"Oh, I'm sorry," Mitch said. "Miss *Sybil.*"

Billie opened her mouth in shock at hearing her full name, then glanced at her dad. He raised his hands in a gesture of surrender, as if to say, "I didn't tell him." Billie closed her eyes for a moment and took a deep breath. Of course Mitch would know her full name—it had probably been on some paperwork she'd had to fill out back when he first hired her. But he'd never used it before. If she showed that it bothered her, Mitch would keep saying it, make it his new favorite bullying trick. Instead of saying anything to Mitch, she turned to her dad, and handed him the fitted sheet that kept falling out of her pile.

"Sure," she told him. "Help me with these fourth-floor rooms, if you would. Maybe I can introduce you to Reno Bridges, if he's around."

"Who?"

Billie turned her back on Mitch and started to tell her dad the story of the dance hall ghost while the elevator carried the two of them upstairs.

Want to know what happens next?
Turn the page for an exclusive excerpt of *Stop, Drop, and Shift*,
Book Three in the Billie Blackwater series.

Find your copy of *Stop, Drop, and Shift* at Amazon,
BarnesandNoble.com, Books-a-Million, or request a copy through
your local independent bookstore.

EXCERPT FROM
STOP, DROP, AND SHIFT
BILLIE BLACKWATER, BOOK THREE

Billie stood across the street from the cabin, ready to watch its destruction. She and Caleb had moved the last of their things out the day before, but had camped out in the sleeping bags on the empty living room floor for one last night. Now, the bulldozers had arrived and the demolition crew was doing some last disconnections and checks before tearing down the cabin and the old livery stable next door.

Caleb squeezed her hand and Billie glanced up at him, grateful he'd agreed to be here with her. The cabin had been Billie's grandmother's; Billie had moved in there at age twelve, after her father accidentally killed her mother and went to prison. Back then, the tiny cabin had felt like a cage that she'd avoided as much as possible, but after her grandmother died and Caleb moved in with her, it had started to feel more like home. They'd lived there together for about three years. But Billie had agreed to sell it in order to save Caleb's life, trading the promise of the sale for the lockbox code of the building where Caleb had been trapped by a monster. Now that bill had come due, and she was unable to put off the sale any longer.

The cabin would be demolished to make room for new shops and hotels along the small mountain town's main street, and Billie had no idea what came next for her and Caleb.

The number of construction workers had doubled since the first ones had knocked on the door that morning. Some of them were on the roof, others on the top floor of the stable, more poking around the perimeter of the property. Finally, they all emerged and some stood back while the others climbed into the bulldozer.

"This is it," Billie whispered, and Caleb held her closer.

But then, nothing happened. The bulldozer didn't roar to life, the wheels stayed stationary, the clawed bucket didn't lift. After several awkward minutes, the bulldozer operator jumped out, leaning down to peer underneath the machine.

Billie and Caleb glanced at each other, then crossed the street to see what was going on. The operator was on the phone, yelling at someone in fast Spanish. When he saw Billie and Caleb approach, he pointed to the ground and asked, "You see who did this?"

"Did what?" Caleb asked.

Billie crouched to look underneath the bulldozer. Oil drained onto the ground like a tiny black waterfall.

"We didn't see anyone," Caleb told the man. The two of them looked at Billie for confirmation. She got back to her feet, lifting her hands in an "I don't know" shrug. She'd lost track of the number of people working around the cabin, about half Juniper locals and half from the out-of-town demolition crew. She definitely hadn't noticed anyone crawling beneath the dozers, but then, she hadn't exactly been watching for that kind of thing.

"Could have been an animal," Billie said. "Squirrels and mice, they get up inside car engines sometimes."

The man scoffed. "No, this was some kind of monkeywrenching bullshit."

Fuel line cut and oil emptied, on both bulldozers. The equipment would have to be towed and replaced before anything else could be done. Billie and Caleb lingered for a little longer, until it became obvious that they were just in the way of the workers.

"Well, that was anticlimactic," Caleb said.

"Strange," Billie said. Their car was loaded with the last of their belongings; she looked around it for anything odd, but no one appeared to have messed with it. "Should we get over to the Silver Coin, then?"

Caleb sighed. He'd spent his adolescence living in his dad's hotel, and Billie knew he was not thrilled about going back there. But for now, they had nowhere else to go.

"Yeah," he relented after a moment. "Let's go finish moving into the Silver Coin."

ABOUT THE AUTHOR

Kira Brinamon grew up in the Rocky Mountains and now lives near the Rio Grande. She holds degrees in Creative Writing from the University of New Mexico and the University of Colorado, Boulder. When not writing, you can often find her at a yoga studio or on a hiking trail. Find her on Twitter @KiraBrinamon or at www.KiraBrinamon.com

ACKNOWLEDGEMENTS

I wrote the lockdown scenes in the fall of 2019, which made for kind of a surreal experience when I was revising this book during the summer of 2020. I did not even realize colloidal silver was being touted as a COVID-19 cure until a few months ago when the body of a cult leader in southern Colorado was found poisoned from it. Funny how the muse hands out things like that sometimes. Anyway, don't take the stuff, yeah? Whether you are a shapeshifter or not.

Before 2020 became what it was, I had intended to road trip to Durango so I could refresh my memory of the setting. Instead, I spent a lot of time looking at Google Images and Pinterest boards to try to work in a more authentic sense of place than I could simply from my own several-year-old memories. So, shout-out to everyone who ever uploaded publicly-available pictures of the town. They were quite helpful when I came up against questions like, "Wait, what kind of piano does the Diamond Belle Saloon have?" and "Does the train actually go under a bridge?"

Once again, massive thank you to the members of my writing group, without whom this book would be a shell of itself.

Thank you for reading!

Please leave an honest review at Amazon, Goodreads, or wherever you discuss books online.

Leaving a review shows support for the author and helps readers like you find new books they'll love.

Please sign up for Kira's newsletter for news about upcoming titles, giveaways, special discounts, & more.

KiraBrinamon.com/newsletter.html